LEAVING the LYREBIRD FOREST

GARY CREW

LEAVING the LYREBIRD FOREST

ILLUSTRATED BY
JULIAN LAFFAN

A Lothian Children's Book

Published in Australia and New Zealand in 2018
by Hachette Australia
Level 17, 207 Kent Street, Sydney NSW 2000
www.hachettechildrens.com.au

10 9 8 7 6 5 4 3 2 1

Text copyright © Gary Crew 2018
Illustrations copyright © Julian Laffan 2018

This book is copyright. Apart from any fair dealing for the purposes of private study, research, criticism or review permitted under the *Copyright Act 1968*, no part may be stored or reproduced by any process without prior written permission.
Enquiries should be made to the publisher.

 A catalogue record for this book is available from the National Library of Australia

ISBN 978 0 7344 1843 2 (paperback)

Cover design by Christabella Designs
Image reproduction by Splitting Image
Author photo courtesy of the author
Illustrator photo courtesy of Katie Tooth
Text design by Bookhouse, Sydney
Typeset in 13.2/20 pt Adobe Garamond Pro by Bookhouse, Sydney
Printed and bound in Australia by McPherson's Printing Group

 The paper this book is printed on is certified against the Forest Stewardship Council® Standards. McPherson's Printing Group holds FSC® chain of custody certification SA-COC-005379. FSC® promotes environmentally responsible, socially beneficial and economically viable management of the world's forests.

For Jane Todd,
who has listened to my moaning with sympathy
Gary

To Orlando,
and all the lyrebirds we have been lucky enough
to see and hear along the way
Julian

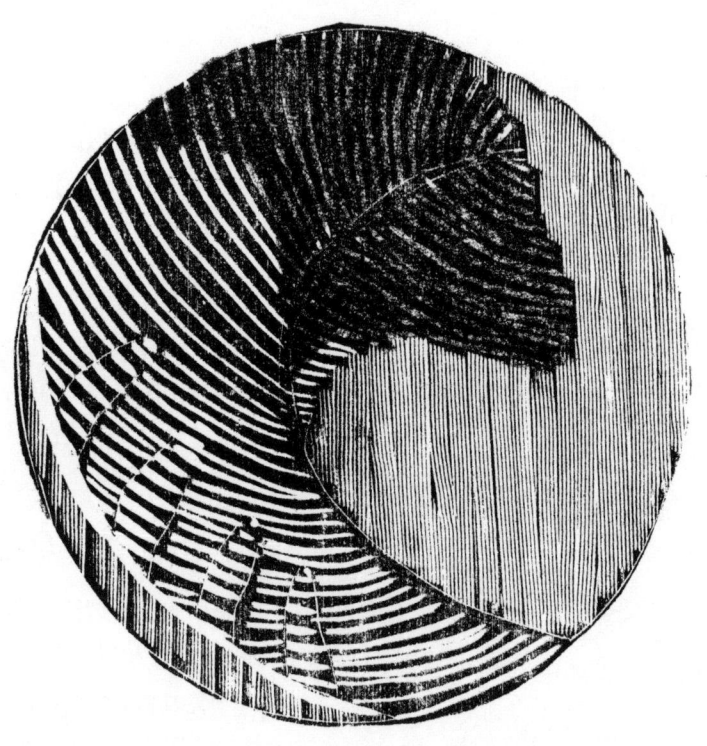

PROLOGUE

The lyrebird forest knows many moods. With the limpid sun, silvery mists rise from the moist earth, languorously piercing lacy tree ferns to vanish, as spirits do, into the lively birdsong of the waking day. At noon, with the sullen sun hammering in molten fury, a heaviness descends – almost a depression – ferns bow, rock mosses shrink and lush grasses wilt. As night descends, stars penetrate the brooding canopy of mountain ash to brush a faery sheen upon all they touch, and the forest is at peace.

CHAPTER ONE

The cedar sash window in Alice Dorritt's bedroom had been handmade by her mother. The curiously warped central pane of transparent glass measured thirty inches by thirty inches; the top left corner boasted a square of dappled ruby, the top right cobalt, also dappled; bottom right an insert of emerald, bottom left, amethyst; at its centre a swirled medallion in the same hue. About the perimeter, connecting these, were strips of citrine, the whole so beautiful it might have formed the illuminated canopy of a royal throne. Through this miracle of design the morning sun struck Alice's auburn hair like a flame.

As a child of three, it was from this window she spotted Birdy, the name that came to her when the lyrebird first visited, pecking on the warped transparent pane.

'*Schmak!*' The sound woke young Alice like some violent alarm. '*Schmak! Schmak!*' – the beak against the glass, again and again – and the girl sat up, alert, the brilliance of the jewelled glass momentarily blinding her until she saw, and bawled, 'Birdy!' The lyrebird turned to look at her, its black claws grappling at her sill. So Alice and the lyrebird met, and the name 'Birdy' stuck.

'Your Birdy is a male,' her father informed her. 'You can tell by his plumage.'

'And if you are lucky, you might see him dance. Even display. When he spreads his tail feathers, they look like a harp. A lyre, some people call it. He is very beautiful. Somewhere there will be a hen, not so pretty, but less vain . . .' her mother laughed.

As the years passed, the bird continued to visit, but only on alternate days. What he did between, other than scratch for worms and centipedes and beetles, remained a mystery. But when Birdy came

tapping on Alice's window (as he was certain to do), she tapped the glass back. Then Birdy would tip his elegant head, his black eyes assessing, as Alice raised the cedar sash until finally, her fingers protruding, she hoped to touch – but the sill was too narrow for the bird to grasp, powerful as his claws were, and he fluttered away.

'Since he is always coming to visit me,' Alice said to her mother, 'Birdy needs a ledge to sit on. He can't perch on the sill. It's too narrow.'

'I'll build a platform,' her mother said. 'Nice and flat and level with your window.'

But when the bird sat on the platform where Alice had spread breadcrumbs and other breakfast dainties, Birdy scratched them away. 'Maybe you have upset him,' her father said. 'Lyrebirds prefer to eat grubs. Put grubs there, and see.'

So the girl scraped some grubs from beneath the bark of a rotting tree but the grubs were also scratched away and when Alice looked, she was certain Birdy had anger in his eyes.

'Can birds be angry?' she asked.

'Who knows what a lyrebird is capable of?' her mother replied. 'They're very intelligent. Did you know they can mimic any sound that they hear?'

'Then I'll test him,' Alice declared. 'I'll test him with sounds. Like Miss Kerr tests how we sound out our alphabet at school.'

When Birdy came, every other morning as he did, and Alice made her sounds through the open window, the bird cocked his head at her and stared, as if she were stupid.

'Birdy hates me,' Alice wailed. 'He only comes because he can see himself in my window. Like all boys, he's vain. Boys were only invented to annoy girls. Miss Kerr says that and I believe her.'

'Perhaps,' Mrs Dorritt mused, nudging her husband. 'Although Miss Kerr is young. Time will tell . . .'

'And that Colin Solomon, the new teller at the bank, has his eye on her, I'm told . . .' Mr Dorritt said with a wink.

These words meant little to Alice, who had no idea, but her parents were right, and time did tell, since all of this happened before the arrival of the bell: the tiny porcelain bell that was to change everything.

CHAPTER TWO

Alice's parents were artists; her father a painter, her mother a sculptor. They had lived in the forest for years. Their rough-hewn workshop could only be discovered by following a tenuous track through the timber. They only 'took to the track' when necessity demanded supplies from the town, a good hour's drive away in their decrepit Model T Ford. But Alice ambled through the trees almost every day to reach the bush school, three miles from her home.

Sometimes as she walked, or wandered on weekends – her hair a red dot among the foliage – Alice wondered what she loved most: the elusive mountain-bird orchid springing up among the fallen leaves, the mysterious hairy fruit of the woolly tea-tree, or the bronze gloss of the swamp skink, liquid to the touch.

'Are you lonely here?' her mother asked.

'Never,' Alice said. 'I've got lots of friends at school. And there's the forest. It's my friend. And there's always Birdy coming to visit. He's my favourite, you know.'

But there was one part of the forest that *did* disturb her; that made her stop and turn, and frown. Perhaps a mile from her home was a turn-off, an even more tenuous track than the one she followed to school, its entrance bearing a weathered wooden sign:

C & M BROWN
NO TRESPASSING

'What does that sign mean?' Alice asked her parents. 'Does someone live down there? I'm not game to go.'

'The Browns built there in the 1920s, a few years after the war,' her father said. 'I believe Mr Brown was granted the land as a returned digger.

To give him a start. That's how this land came to us too, through my father. Like us, the Browns don't want to be disturbed. We haven't seen them much since you were a baby. Mrs Brown brought woollen booties for you. I believe she spun the wool herself. Mr Brown takes his handcraft to town in his dray sometimes. He sells it at the market.'

'If I stop at that sign and stand very still, I sometimes hear voices,' Alice confessed. 'But they sound eerie through the bush and I'm too spooked to get closer.'

'I would leave them alone,' her mother advised. 'Evidently they're content and, as you know, we all find happiness in our own way.'

Alice nodded. 'I understand,' she said. 'They must be very old. I'll leave them in peace because I'm happy here too.'

CHAPTER THREE

BEING ARTISTS, THE DORRITTS WERE FAR FROM wealthy, making a meagre living from the occasional sale of their work. They had a cow called Bessie, some goats (Alice didn't like their wobbly lips that nibbled), a dog that was never home, a few chooks and a vegetable patch. Theirs was a simple life and so, as Alice's ninth birthday approached, Gwen Dorritt announced the inevitable.

'Alice,' she said, 'we can't afford any flash presents, but I can make you a very nice cake. What sort would you like?'

'A sponge cake,' Alice said. 'With strawberries and cream. But no candles. I don't like candles. They burn out and die.'

'We all burn out and die,' her father yelled from another room. 'It's called mortality!'

'Shush, Ernie, you're not being helpful! This is Alice's birthday, not a funeral,' Mrs Dorritt yelled back. 'Well, Miss Alice, on a cheerier note, I have the makings for the cake and the cream – bless our Bessie's udder! – but not the strawberries . . .'

Alice's face fell.

'But . . .' her mother added very quickly, 'your father's run out of viridian tint and burnt sienna in his watercolours and really should take the Ford into town. Maybe –'

'Please?'

'Consider it done. Winsor and Newton viridian tint and burnt sienna watercolours *and* big fat strawberries it is. Ernie, did you hear that?'

'I heard,' Mr Dorritt answered. 'Alice's wish is my command.'

There were enough struggling artists in the area to support a craft supplier (only just). As Ernie Dorritt left the shop, paints (and strawberries) under his arm to return to his car in the paddock out back, he spotted a Country Women's Association charity stall, tempting bric-a-brac spread on a cambric cloth of dazzling white.

He could not resist.

'Good morning, Mrs Goodenough,' he said, tipping his hat. 'And what have we here?'

'Oh, these were mostly my mother-in-law's things,' Mrs Goodenough sighed, simultaneously raising her eyes to a passing cloud and dabbing a hankie, redolent with eau de cologne, to her powdered cleavage. 'Gone, she is. Gone . . .' though no further clouds appeared for her to dwell upon.

'I am sorry,' Ernie said. 'You will miss her.'

'I will, but life must go on. And hubby and myself aren't well off, you know. So . . .' and she spread her chubby fingers to indicate the trinkets.

Ernie looked, remembering Alice's birthday. There were many lace doilies, many bead-edged milk jug covers, many sherry glasses (the elderly

Mrs Goodenough had loved her tipple); but there, in the middle of the not-for-Alice stuff, sat a bell.

Leaning forward, Ernie picked it up to cradle in his palm. 'This is a pretty thing,' he said.

'Ah,' Mrs Goodenough sighed. 'As I said, that was my mother-in-law's. It sat on her bedside table and when she needed me, or a pick-me-up . . .' she tapped an upturned sherry glass with a yellowing fingernail, 'she would ring. It's porcelain, you understand. Not common china. Bavarian porcelain. With a peacock feather wrapping around, hand-painted, you see. Very delicate, for five shillings . . .' and she waited, hoping for a cloud.

Ernie Dorritt did indeed see, but what he saw was not a hand-painted, wrapping-around peacock feather, but the tail feather of a lyrebird, and five shillings or ten shillings or a paper note, this pretty thing would belong to Alice.

'I will have that,' he said, perhaps too adamantly, and reaching for his coin purse, he added, 'do you have any tissue paper? It's very fine.'

'I do,' Mrs Goodenough beamed. 'And Sellotape.'

So the bell was wrapped and, having been bound in tape, popped into Ernie Dorritt's pocket, where it nestled, as if at home already.

The birthday morning was an alternate day, so Birdy did not come tapping, nor was he expected, but the delivery of marmalade jam on butter-dripping toast (thank you, Bessie's udder) was a treat for Alice. Better yet, when Mrs Dorritt put the kettle on at ten o'clock, out came the cake. Three layers of sponge (three!), with cream and strawberries between and even more cream and freshly halved strawberries on top, all glistening with caster sugar.

'Yum, yum, chookie's bum!' Alice gloated.

Then her father produced his gift, still wrapped in yards of Sellotape.

'What is this?' Alice asked, unwrapping and unwrapping, until finally, the bell was revealed. 'It's beautiful,' she declared, holding it to the light. 'Translucent even . . .'

'Translucent!' her mother exclaimed. 'That's a new word.'

'Miss Kerr is a good teacher,' Alice replied, glancing back. 'And I forgot to tell you, she's engaged to be married. To Mr Solomon, from the bank, who's very handsome, so she says . . .'

'Never!' Gwen Dorritt laughed, winking at her husband. 'Well, there you go!'

But the bell could not be ignored, and holding the fragile handle – also made of porcelain – Alice shook it, ever so lightly, filling the room with one pure note.

'Oh!' she said. 'It's so clear – not tinny or tinkly – just right. I don't know how to describe it. The sound is so *true*!'

Gwen Dorritt raised her eyebrows. How gifted was this girl? 'I think you have described it very well,' she said. 'Truly.'

'And there's a feather painted on it,' Alice said. 'Going right around. Did you paint that, Dad?'

'No,' he admitted. 'I did not, but look carefully. What sort of feather is it?'

'A lyrebird's tail feather?'

'It is. You see them best when the bird displays. I couldn't resist it.'

'I've read about how lyrebirds display,' Alice said, 'but I've never seen one. I mean, I've never seen Birdy bow and spread his tail. Not once.'

'One day you will,' her father promised, giving Alice a hug. 'Oooops,' he chuckled, almost upsetting the plate of birthday cake in her hand. 'Now, don't eat too much cake. We don't want you getting sick. You have a Geography test tomorrow.'

'Thanks, Dad,' Alice said. 'And thank you for my bell. I'll put it on my bedside table. Since I've failed to get Birdy's attention any other way, I'll test its sound on him in the morning – *before* Miss Kerr tests my Geography.' Clutching the bell and her cake plate, she headed for her room.

CHAPTER FOUR

Next morning Alice woke to the '*Schmak! Schmak! Schmaking!*' of Birdy's beak against her window.

'Morning, Birdy,' she said. 'Today is my Geography test, but I also have a test for you . . .' Slipping out of bed, she reached for the porcelain bell and crossed to the window. Birdy eyed her, askance. Holding the bell high, Alice shook it to produce that one true note.

Birdy stood on the ledge, gaping, then, lifting his head to expose his elegant throat, he repeated the sound. Faultless. Exact. Pure.

'Wonderful!' Alice cried. 'Birdy, you're wonderful!'

Knowing his own worth, Birdy bowed.

'Again,' Alice said. 'Let's do it again.' Raising the bell, she rang it once more.

Birdy responded, repeating the sound three times as if to say, 'There! I got that right,' and Alice stood back from the window, laughing.

'You've passed your test,' Alice cried. 'In fact, you've come top! Miss Kerr would be delighted.' Scuttling out of the room, she called her parents.

When Ernie and Gwen Dorritt had been arranged beside her bed, facing the window, Alice announced, 'This performance will be presented for your amusement by Miss Alice Dorritt and Master Birdy Lyrebird, to the tune of a porcelain bell. Are you ready?'

Her parents nodded.

At the sound of the bell, Birdy responded with three pure notes and, performance complete, leapt from his ledge to disappear into the scrub.

'Bravo!' Gwen Dorritt cried.

'Super-dooper,' Ernie Dorritt applauded.

'But now,' Alice announced, looking grave, 'I must have my brekkie and get to school. Today's my Geography test. Remember?'

CHAPTER FIVE

Since the Dorritts lived an isolated life in the forest, Alice attended the tiny primary school in the town nearby. The pity was, in two years' time – once she reached fourteen – she would have to leave that school and her friendships would be broken up as each child either found a job or chose a high school or boarding school. Alice would miss her favourite teacher, Miss Kerr – who still hadn't married Colin Solomon, despite his amorous displays. *I don't really want to go to boarding school*, Alice thought as she wandered through the bush. I certainly don't want to leave the forest, especially Birdy, but I want a career – something to do with nature, or native animals, or lyrebirds – but the nearest proper boarding school is miles away . . . On this melancholy note, she stooped to pick up a twig. *But it's too soon to worry about that, I suppose*, she reconsidered, *since I'm only twelve*. So she loitered, bending to sniff flowers or collect fallen leaves, her fiery hair appearing and reappearing through the scrub like a dash of red paint in a landscape.

One afternoon, as Alice dawdled home, on reaching the turn-off to the Brown place, she paused (as she often did) to listen. At first, she heard nothing, which was not unusual, but as she turned to wander on, a curious sound caught her attention.

A muffled sob, was it?

She stopped.

There it was again. Surely, deep in the bush, along the 'C & M Brown' track, someone was weeping.

I must go down there, Alice thought. *I must*, and, tightening her leather satchel, she turned down the rutted path.

Maybe a hundred yards along, she stopped again. Yes, someone was crying. So she went on, nervous but determined, until through a clearing in the forest she saw a weatherboard house – its timbers grey and unpainted – raised on stumps a few feet off the ground. Timber steps led up to a verandah. There, on the top step, sat an old man, his grey head in his hands, weeping.

Alice did not hesitate. 'Mister,' she called, 'are you all right?'

He looked up, wiping his nose with the back of his hand, searching for the source of the voice.

'Are you all right?' Alice repeated, moving to the bottom of the stairs.

When he saw her, he stood, half turning towards the door as if to leave, but she called, 'No. Don't go. What's the matter?'

He looked back. She saw that he was old – grandfather old, like in one of her picture books – but his face was kind. He tried to smile and she said, 'I'm Alice Dorritt. I'm your neighbour from down the track.'

'Hello,' he said, sitting down again on the top step. 'I'm sorry I was rude, but she's gone and I

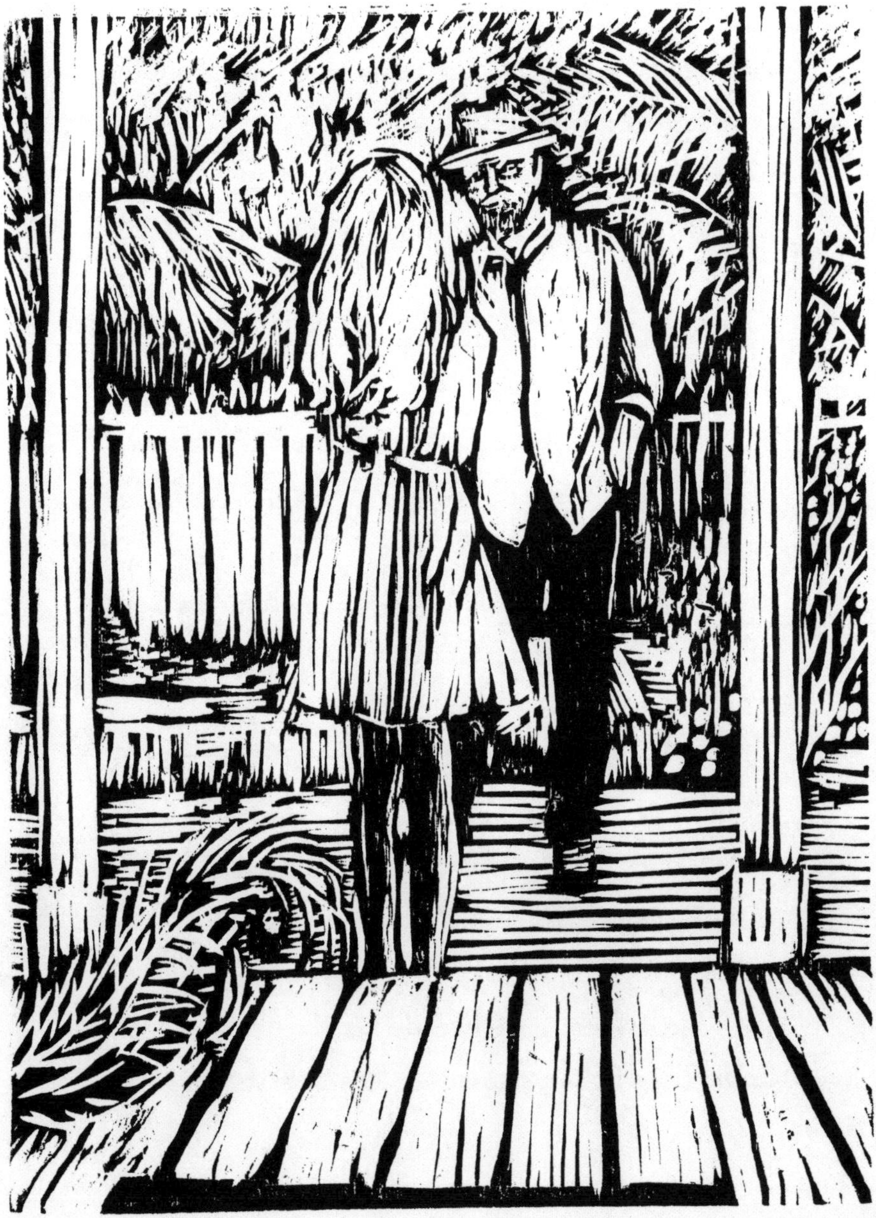

can't get used to it.' He turned his head, looking wistfully into the scrub.

Alice followed his gaze, expecting a dog to appear, or maybe a cow, but saw nothing. 'Who's gone?' she asked.

'Marcella,' he said. 'My wife. She passed away a month ago.'

'I'm sorry,' Alice mumbled, then added, awkwardly, 'So she is the "M"?'

'Pardon?'

'Is Marcella the "M" on the sign at the start of the path? And are you the "C"?'

'What?'

'The sign at the start of the path: "C and M Brown". Who is the "C"?'

'That's me. Cyril Brown. I'm so sorry. I'm not thinking straight. And I'm being rude. What did you say your name was?'

'Alice Dorritt. I live down the way . . .' she pointed, 'with my parents. They're artists.'

'Ah,' he sighed. 'The Dorritts. Yes, I remember. Marcella has been sick for so long, I've ignored my neighbours. I apologise.' He stood and turned as if to go in, but changed his mind. 'Um . . . Alice,' he said, turning back, 'can I offer you a drink? I make my own lemonade from bush lemons. It's good.'

Alice thought for a moment. It would be polite to stay since Mr Brown was sad and probably in need of friends. 'Yes, thank you,' she said. 'I'd like that,' and she climbed the steps to stand beside him.

'Do come in,' he invited.

Only then did she catch sight of the open front door and the eerie darkness beyond. Her stomach dropped. She didn't know this man. Seeing the airy width of the verandah stretching to her right and left, with its inviting table and chairs, she said, 'Oh, I'll wait here. It's so nice.' She sank into the nearest chair, her leather satchel on her knee.

Mr Brown nodded and disappeared into the depths of the house.

Alice looked around. Although the house was only a mile or so from her place, the fact that it was raised on those funny wooden stumps gave her a different outlook on the bush. She was looking down into it, not straight at it, as she did through her bedroom window.

When Mr Brown reappeared, he carried a wooden tray, carved all over with gumnuts and blossoms. On this was a pottery jug of lemonade and two glasses. He placed the tray carefully on a wicker table beside Alice. 'Thank you,' she said. 'I was wondering, did you build this house?'

'No,' he laughed. 'I had a land grant as a returned soldier after the war. With the money Marcella and I had saved, we chose this design from a catalogue. It's called the "Dalby": a Queensland-style house, hence the stumps to let cool air under in the summer and the wide verandahs on all four sides. We loved the verandahs – and with every room opening onto them through full-length

French doors, we could look out onto the bush almost like we lived in a tree house.'

She watched him as he spoke. He *did* have a nice face: open and friendly, and a nice smile, and blue eyes. She liked blue eyes. Hers were what her father called 'muddy river', which meant they were a kind of browny-green. As she drank the delicious lemonade, she asked, 'And did you work? Or do you work?'

'I was a postman before the war,' he said. 'Delivering letters on a pushbike. After the war, I was promoted to postmaster at Lilydale. That's how I saved the money for this house. But I'm old now and retired.'

'You must do something,' Alice insisted. 'Do you have any hobbies?'

'I read. And I do my pokerwork,' he said. 'I take the dray into town once a week to collect any mail. I watch the bush. The wildlife.'

Alice didn't know what pokerwork was but she said nothing. Since she did so well at school, she was not about to admit her ignorance on any topic.

'Well,' she said, finishing her drink, 'it's been nice to talk but Mum and Dad will be worried. I really should go. I'm glad I met you at last.' Standing, she shook his hand. 'Goodbye, Mr Brown.'

'Goodbye, Alice,' he answered. 'I'm sorry I was so miserable.'

'You have good reason,' she smiled, though as she made her way down the front steps a sudden shiver passed over her as she remembered the gloom of the depths of the house. Was it the spirit of Marcella that bothered her, she wondered as she walked home. *I'll ask Mum*, she resolved, and hurried on.

CHAPTER SIX

'He gave me lemonade that he made himself,' Alice told her mother as she gobbled a plate of peanut bickies. 'And he said that he had a hobby called "pokerwork". What does that mean?'

'Pokerwork is a kind of cottage craft, mostly practised by men,' Mrs Dorritt explained. 'Usually they use a heated wire or "poker" to burn a design into timber, much like I've seen you do with a magnifying glass, catching the sun's rays and burning a hole in paper. Did Mr Brown show you anything that he'd made?'

'He did – but he didn't. The tray he served the lemonade on was decorated all over with gumnuts and flowers that looked like they'd been burnt into the wood. What a dill I am. I didn't know. It was beautiful. So Mr Brown is an artist too.'

'And did he show you around his house?'

Alice almost choked on a biscuit. 'You mean, did I go inside? No.'

'So where did you have the lemonade?'

'On the front verandah. That was really nice. The house looked scary inside. Dark and gloomy. Like Marcella Brown was still there.'

'But you just said that she was dead.'

'That's what I mean.'

'I don't understand.'

'I felt like her ghost was lurking in the dark. Inside the house looked creepy. I was scared.'

'That's the silliest thing I've ever heard.'

Alice hung her head. 'I should go back, shouldn't I?' she groaned. 'I should take Mr Brown something to cheer him up. Some cheese maybe? I didn't see a cow or a goat.'

'I'll make him a cake,' Mrs Dorritt decided. 'Now go and wash up for dinner.'

The following Sunday afternoon, while the sleepy bush droned with the hum of cicadas, Alice took cake and cheese to Mr Brown. She climbed the stairs bravely and knocked at the open door without once succumbing to her lurking fears. 'There is no such thing as ghosts. Sorry, Marcella,' she whispered under her breath and then, he was there: Mr Cyril Brown himself, all smiles and wrinkles, evidently delighted to see her.

'Alice!' he declared. 'How wonderful. Do come in . . .' and she stepped fearlessly inside. Mr Brown took the cake and cheese to the kitchen while Alice looked around.

Since the interior was so dark, and she had moved from the bright sunlight of the verandah into gloom, Alice half expected to enter a hallway but, as her eyes adjusted, she found herself in a large room.

'This is the living room,' Mr Brown told her when he returned. 'We hardly use it but it's like the heart of the house and all the other rooms open off it. I want to show you the bush from the back verandah. It's much thicker, as you'll see.'

Though intimidated by the darkened room, Alice was fascinated. She paused, looking about.

Mr Brown waited.

The walls were stained timber, rather than painted, with dilapidated lounge chairs covered in brown fabric nestled in the corners. Above the doors opening off all sides were fret-work lunettes of kangaroos and emus facing off as if they were in a boxing ring. By the fractured light these lunettes allowed in, Alice could make out occasional tables and multi-tiered whatnots, each cluttered with bric-a-brac on crochet doilies. Here and there glimmered a brass jardinière (which somebody must have polished, once), and in the middle, on a low table, a heavy bottle-green vase containing what looked like six or eight elegant feathers.

'Are they lyrebird feathers?' Alice asked.

'Yes,' he answered. 'From time to time, Marcella found their feathers in the bush.'

'A lyrebird visits our house,' Alice said, but Mr Brown had moved on, appearing not to have heard.

Ghosts aside (who believed in ghosts?), this was a forbidding room, and unwelcoming. *Someone should open those doors and let in some light*, Alice thought. *I would get claustrophobia trapped in here.* Then she spotted the framed pictures hanging on the walls.

'Oh!' she exclaimed. 'Can I look? Mum and Dad are both artists. I like to look at art . . .' But when she stood on tiptoe and looked closely, she found the images morbid. They were mounted in dark timber frames and suspended on wires from hooks attached to a narrow board running right around the room, about two feet below the ceiling. The first was of a stag with huge antlers, standing alone and looking melancholy on a mountain peak. The second showed a child's pale hand protruding from a snowdrift and a collie dog, head back, howling as if to let somebody

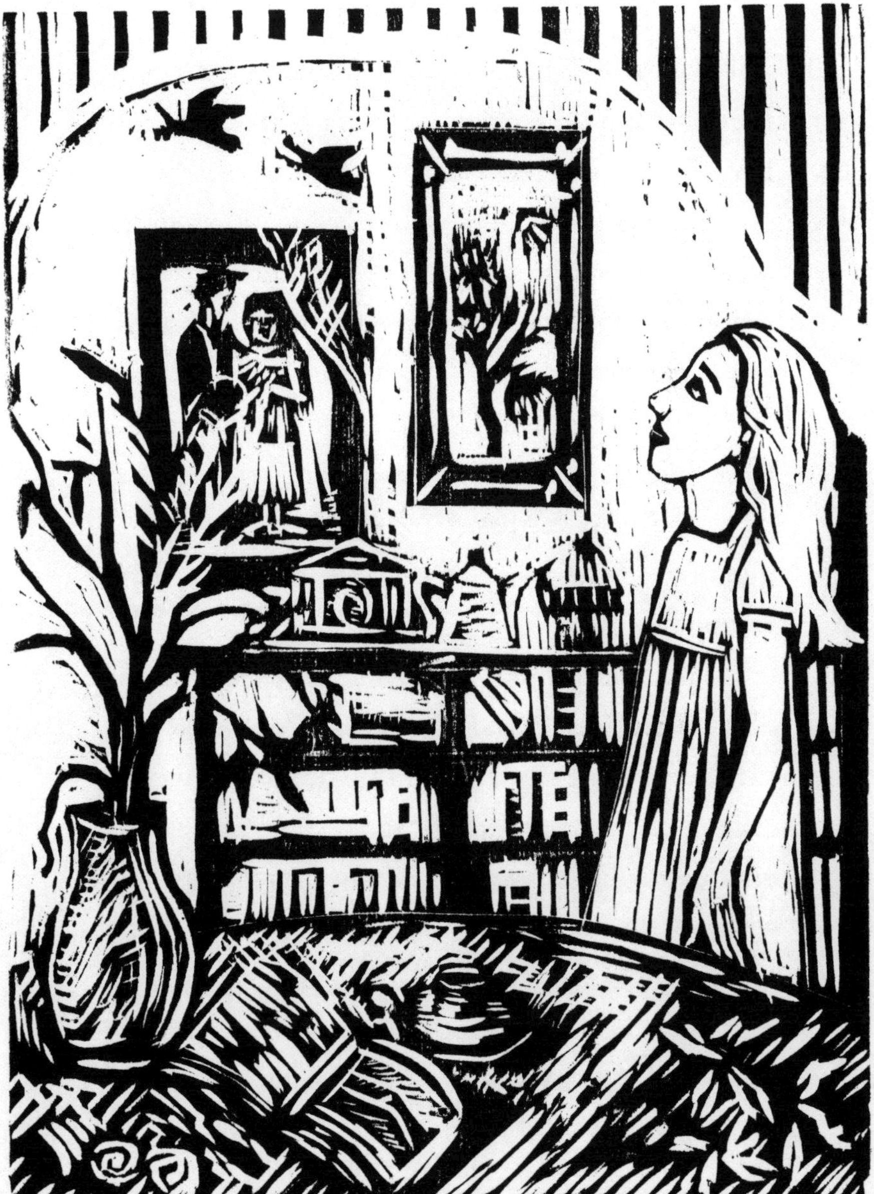

know what it had discovered. *Ugh!* Alice thought. Not only are they prints – her parents had taught her to despise prints – they're depressing. Awful! And finally, she stopped before a sepia photograph of a sober wedding party. 'That's our big day,' Mr Brown said, cheerily. 'That's me and Marcella and her sister, Elsie, our bridesmaid.'

'She was so young. And so pretty,' Alice said, which the bride was, in a pale and terrified kind of way. 'And you were handsome . . .' she added, giggling. 'But why is all that yellow net around the photo?'

'Ah,' Mr Brown sighed. 'That's her wedding veil. It's old now. It was pure white. You can see the tiny wax orange blossoms set into it. So long ago. So long . . . Come now, let me show you the back . . .' and, taking her elbow, he led her through the house towards the back door. On the way, she caught a glimpse of the kitchen. In a far corner lurked an enormous cast-iron wood-burning stove, kindling piled beside it. A scrubbed pine table dominated the room, littered with willow pattern cups and saucers and stacks of plates and crusts and bottles of jam and half-eaten biscuits. In the middle of the table was an uncovered jug of milk. Even at a glance, Alice could see a fly struggling on the milk's surface. *Oh dear*, she thought, *Mr Brown is not looking after himself. He needs some help.*

The rear door was closed (why, Alice couldn't imagine) but when Mr Brown opened it, she gasped: they were in the forest; the tree fern fronds draped over the verandah rails right there, the mountain ash rearing so close she could stroke their silken bark.

'This is beautiful,' Alice exclaimed. 'Just like living in a tree house, like you said.'

'Yes. And that's the very reason we chose this house design. It's so open to the bush.'

Alice could not resist: 'But since it's so open to the bush, why do you keep the doors shut? Inside is so dark.'

Mr Brown laughed. 'What you've seen is pretty dark,' he admitted. 'But you've only seen the living room. The reason we keep the doors shut is because, lovely as they are, the tree ferns scatter their spore everywhere.'

'Spore? What's spore?'

'Seeds. Millions of them. Like dust. And it covers everything. It drove Marcella crazy. So we shut the doors. But the other rooms are different. They're light as air. They all have full-length French doors. We'll have a cup of tea and some of your lovely cake and I'll show you. Okay?'

'Okay,' Alice agreed. 'But can we have our afternoon tea out here? I mean, our place is surrounded by bush too – and tree ferns, of course – but we're not living in them like you are.'

'I know. I know,' Mr Brown chuckled. 'Come on. Let's eat!'

But after two pieces of chocolate cake (each!) and having talked her head off (nearly . . .), Alice said, 'Mr Brown, it's Sunday and I have some homework to finish for tomorrow. Can I come back another day? I could help with the housework, you know. Would you mind?'

'Mind?' he laughed. 'I'm hopeless at housework. Marcella did all of that. My dear, you're the best thing that's happened to me for ages. You can come by anytime. I'll be here. And we can talk – and eat cake – to our hearts' content . . .'

CHAPTER SEVEN

So Alice slipped into the habit of visiting Mr Brown – sometimes on the way home from school, sometimes on weekends – and as they sat on the verandah one Saturday afternoon (having devoured far too many cream-filled butterfly cakes – thanks, Mrs Dorritt and Bessie's udder!), out of the blue Mr Brown announced, 'Well, it's time you saw the rest of the house . . . but I have to tell you something first.'

'What's that?' Alice asked, intrigued.

'We had a son,' Mr Brown blurted out. 'Once. Marcella and I,' he looked away. 'His name was Ronald – and maybe still is. Who knows?' Then he was silent, looking down at his hands, his fingers clenching and unclenching in his lap.

Seeing his suffering, Alice said, 'Mr Brown, we don't have to talk about this. Honest.'

'But I want to,' he said. 'In fact, I have to if we're to become real friends. Ronald was a big part of our lives. I know that Marcella has passed away, but Ron simply vanished. Up and gone. I don't know where. Or why . . .'

'I'm listening,' Alice said.

'I'm telling you this because when I show you around the house, you'll see that we've kept his room exactly as it was from when he was little.' Standing, he led her through the living room. 'This is Ron's room,' he said, opening a door to his left.

'Oh!' Alice gasped as light flooded the space. 'I hadn't expected . . .' Immediately before her were glass doors reaching from floor to ceiling. These were draped with delicate lace curtains and beyond them, the lacy foliage of tree fern and gum hung languidly over the verandah. Sunlight fell in dazzling patches across the bare timber floor, the single bed and the thousand and one items of boyhood that Alice saw before her.

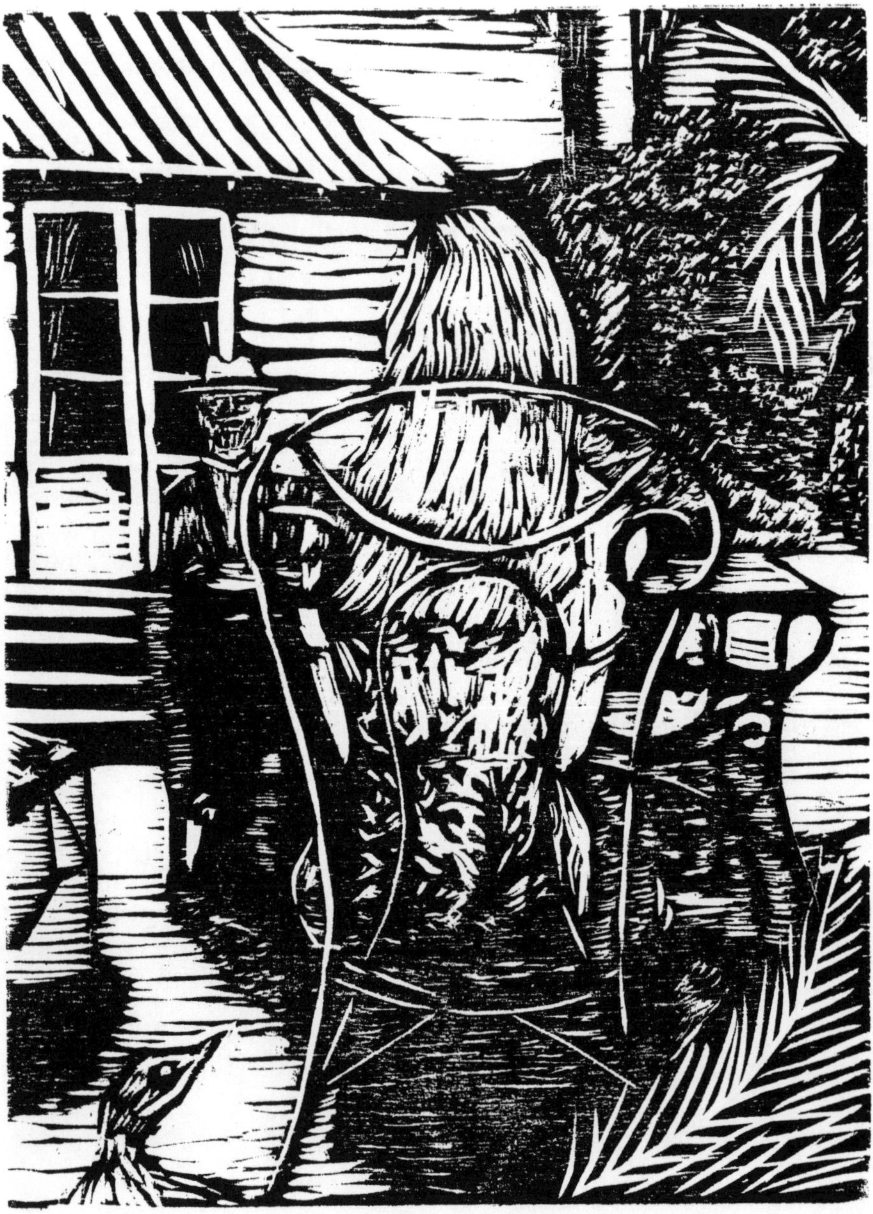

'Ron left almost twenty years ago,' Mr Brown said, casting his arms wide as if to reveal the room's wonders. 'Just up and left. To go where, we don't know.'

Alice gaped. Before her were jigsaw puzzles, Meccano sets in tin boxes, Build-it construction bricks, cricket bats and stumps . . . every conceivable toy a boy could want – all blotched and dappled by that lacy light.

'But why would any boy leave this?' Alice asked. 'It's like an Aladdin's cave . . .'

There was the perfectly made bed (its cover embroidered with ferns), a beautiful red cedar lowboy with three drawers, a full-length cheval mirror with a cricket cap hooked on one post and a digger's hat on the other. And books! There were shelves piled with novels and comics.

'It looks like he was a sports nut *and* a reader,' Alice said, tentatively perusing the books. Turning to Mr Brown, she repeated, 'Why would any boy leave this? I don't understand.'

'We're always hoping that . . .' Mr Brown turned away, embarrassed.

'He isn't . . .' Alice couldn't say 'dead', but Mr Brown worked that out.

'No. Ron's not dead. At least I don't think so. He came here with us when we built the house but he never liked the isolation. Sure, he would take his books and sit on the verandah and read by himself. Like you, he had no brothers or sisters and he only saw other kids when he went to school – just like you, as I say – but he longed for company and as he grew older, he started riding his bike into town and catching the train to the city. That's when he really got itchy feet. Sometimes – well, lots of times, and more and more often – he didn't come home at night. We were sick with worry.' He picked up the cricket cap and fondled it lovingly. 'Marcella and I couldn't sleep, and then finally, when he was seventeen, Ron stopped coming home at all.'

'Did he find a job?'

Mr Brown put the cap back onto the mirror's post and hung his head. 'I have no idea. He vanished into thin air. We notified the police but that came to nothing and now, after all these years, I'm still none the wiser.'

'He never wrote you a letter?'

'Not a word. So now you know. Come on. I'll show you my workroom. It's cheerier. I thought that you should know about Ron. He's still with us – well, me anyway – as you can see . . .' and showing Alice into the living room, he closed the door.

But Alice was not satisfied. *Why would a boy – a man, was he, at seventeen? – leave all his treasures, his family home, his loving parents, just like that?* Deep in thought, she stopped to touch the lyre-bird feathers, musing: *where are you, Mr Birdy? Are these your feathers?* She turned to Mr Brown, asking, 'Um . . . I know that it's none of my business, but did Ron take anything with him when he left?'

'One thing and one thing only,' Mr Brown replied. 'His stamp album.'

'His stamp album?' Alice repeated incredulously.

'His stamp album,' Mr Brown sighed.

'So maybe he wanted to see the world,' Alice said.

Apparently unwilling or unable to reply, Mr Brown opened the next door, announcing: 'This is my workroom. I spend most of my time in here, now that I'm alone.'

Alice stepped inside.

This room had the same French doors as Ron's but without the lace curtains. Since it was uncovered, the clear glass gave an uninterrupted view of the scrub and, Alice noted with some amusement that the panes were warped and wobbly just like the sash window in her bedroom, without the jewelled inserts.

This certainly was a workroom. From either side of the French doors timber benches stretched around the walls. These benches were littered with tools and tape measures and bottles full of nails and screws and tins of paint and all sorts of brushes and lengths of timber and cans of paraffin oil and a thousand and one other bits and pieces peculiar to a craftsman's den.

'This is where I do my pokerwork,' Mr Brown announced proudly.

Alice looked about then asked, 'Can you show me what you do?'

Mr Brown beamed. 'It would be my pleasure,' he said. He reached for a piece of flat yellow wood. 'I draw a design on a piece of timber, like this one; maybe a gum leaf, say – and I light this . . .' He picked up what looked like a tin can with a long thin nozzle sticking out of the top. 'This is filled with benzene, or sometimes paraffin. I light the fumes to burn the shape I've drawn into the wood.'

'So why is it called pokerwork?'

'Because in this nozzle sticking out is a piece of stiff wire that glows red hot in the flame from the benzene fumes. It's like a red-hot poker that burns into the wood.'

'And these are some of the things you've made?' Alice asked, picking up wooden vases and trays decorated with kookaburras and leaves and gumnuts.

'That's what I do. I take them into town and sell them at the little craft market.'

But as Alice put the items he had made back on the bench near the windows, she happened to glance outside and there, bolted to the verandah railing, was a wooden platform just like the one her mother had made for Birdy.

'Mr B,' she called, pointing, 'what's that platform on the verandah for?'

'Ah!' he laughed. 'That is where Fred sits when he visits.'

'Fred?'

'Fred's one very special bird. A lyrebird in fact. Apart from you, Fred is my best friend.'

'A lyrebird?' Alice nearly choked. 'Really?'

'Oh, there are lots of lyrebirds in this forest. But Fred is special. He visits every other morning. Like clockwork.' But he didn't finish because Alice had opened the doors and stepped out onto the verandah.

'What are you looking for?' Mr Brown asked.

Alice smiled, a little shamefaced. 'I was just wondering if I might spot my Birdy,' she said.

'My Birdy?' Mr Brown repeated, following her. 'Who's my Birdy?'

'It's too hard to explain,' Alice said, 'but I need to ask, has Fred come to see you today?'

Mr Brown frowned. 'Well, yes. This morning as a matter of fact. Every other day, as I said. At half past six. I feed him grubs on his platform. Sometimes he eats them, sometimes he doesn't but –'

'Mr B,' Alice said, 'can I come back at half past six the day *after* tomorrow? That's Monday morning. Would you mind?'

'Mind? Of course not. You're welcome anytime. But why?'

'Let's just say I have a test for Fred,' and she slipped away.

CHAPTER EIGHT

Sunday morning Alice woke to the '*Schmak! Schmak! Schmaking!* of Birdy's beak against her window. As usual, she sat up and welcomed him. 'Good morning, Birdy,' she said. 'Or should I be calling you Fred?'

The bird cocked its head to one side and blinked, as if trying to comprehend.

Alice giggled. 'Come on,' she encouraged. 'Do you go to Mr Brown's on the mornings that you don't visit me? And are you Fred there and Birdy here? You can tell me. We're friends, aren't we? And friends share secrets.'

'Have it your way, then,' she said, reaching for the porcelain bell on her bedside table. 'But I'm going to test you like Miss Kerr tests us. I need to find out if you're who I think you are – or if you have a twin called Fred.'

She rang the bell, sounding one true note and, naturally enough, the bird replied with a single note, equally true.

'Ah!' Alice declared. 'You know that bell-note off by heart, don't you? But let me warn you: tomorrow morning, bright and early, I'll be on Mr Brown's verandah to test the bird that visits his place. Perhaps you will be there – perhaps you won't. That's a joke. Ha! Ha!'

Once Birdy had eaten a few grubs and vanished into the scrub, Alice spent a quiet Sunday. First, she helped her mother bake patty cakes (well, she coated them with wild passionfruit icing, then licked the spoon!); she went for a lazy walk; she idly threw some pebbles in the bit of creek that trickled through the bush behind their house, then hopped onto her bed to read a few more chapters of Arthur Ransome's novel *Swallows and Amazons* because she loved the untamed (though oh, so romantic) idea of the Lake District. After she'd taken a nap, she invaded the kitchen to check what was on offer for dinner.

A lazy day indeed.

Early next morning, Mr Brown heard knocking on his front door. Guessing it was Alice, he opened it with a welcoming smile. 'Come in, my friend,' he said. 'I wondered if you would make it so early. What are you doing about going to school?'

Alice slipped her leather schoolbag from her shoulders and put it on the verandah by the front door. 'You know my mother made that bag,' she said. 'Mum's very clever. See how she's tooled a lyrebird into the flap? I packed it last night and made Vegemite sandwiches for breakfast so I'm all ready to go. If I get to school at half past seven, Miss Kerr will be there. She's another early bird ... Early *bird*, get it? That was a joke, Mr B.'

Mr Brown gave her a wondering look. 'Alice,' he began, 'what's all of this about? And what did you mean when you said that you have a test for my Fred?'

Alice didn't answer. Rather, she knelt to open her schoolbag. 'Can I come in?' she asked. 'But first, tell me, has Fred visited yet?'

'No,' Mr Brown replied, 'although he will. He always does. Every other day, like I said. You're welcome to meet him, if that's what you want.'

'Good,' she said. 'And I'll need to go into your workroom to apply my test, if that's okay.' Standing, she held out a tiny parcel wrapped in tissue paper.

'Come in by all means,' Mr Brown said. 'What's the mystery? And what's that in your hand?'

'You'll see,' she assured him, as she entered his room.

Mr Brown stood by the door, scratching his head as Alice moved straight to the French doors, her eyes fixed on the feeding platform attached to the verandah rail outside. 'Is Fred very shy?'

'Find out for yourself,' Mr Brown laughed. 'There he is now. I'm guessing that he won't be too happy because his food isn't spread out for him. My preparation of his breakfast was interrupted when I showed you in.'

Alice opened the French door, and began to ease out, very slowly. 'He sure looks like Birdy,' she whispered.

'What?' Mr Brown wondered. 'Looks like who?'

Alice turned to Mr Brown again as the bird sprang onto the feeding platform and strutted about in a vain search for food. 'Let me apply the test,' Alice said, and removing her porcelain bell from the tissue in her hand she rang it once.

The bird stopped dithering immediately and looked up. Staring directly at Alice, it raised its elegant head to call: and the call was the sound of the bell in her hand – the one true note Alice knew so well.

'Mr B,' she gasped, 'I call this lyrebird Birdy, but you call him Fred. He's been coming to my bedroom window since I was a little girl. And this,' she held out the bell, 'is the test I put him to;

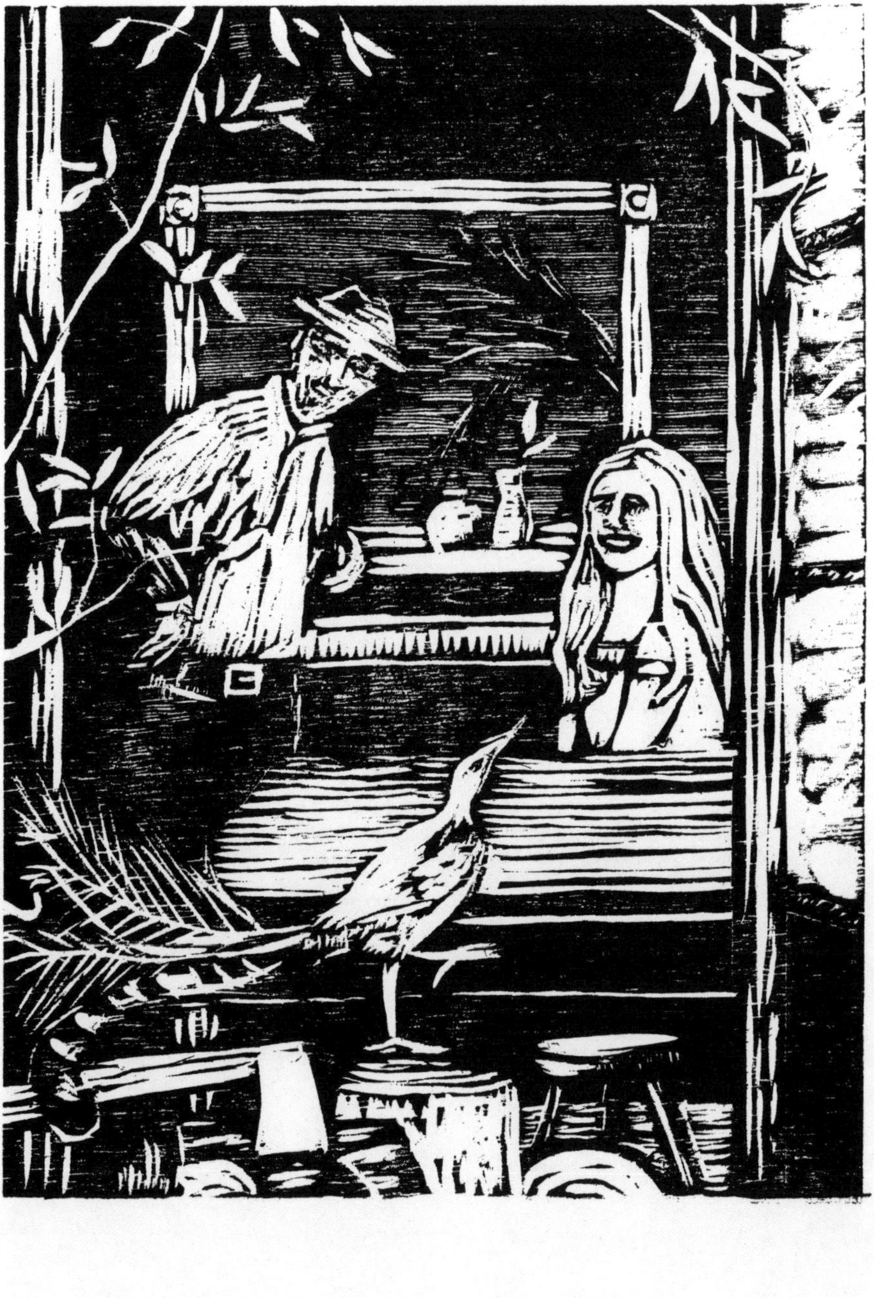

to hear if he could mimic the sound of the bell that he hears every other morning – that is, when he's not visiting you as his alter ego Fred – and he's passed with flying colours.'

'Well, well,' Mr Brown muttered, stepping onto the verandah. 'Fred, you naughty bird, aren't my grubs and weevils good enough? Do you have to go to the neighbours and get your sweeties from them? Tell me?' He knelt on the verandah below the platform. As soon as he did, the bird hopped to the edge and peered down, then, as if to prove what he'd learnt from Alice, he threw back his head and made the bell sound three times – each call clear and true.

'Stone the crows,' Mr Brown said. 'I believe he is your Birdy, Alice. Fred has never made that sound for me. It's beautiful. Really beautiful.'

'But you probably never gave Fred any reason to make that sound,' Alice pointed out. 'Have you tried different sounds on him?'

Mr Brown looked away, suddenly sheepish.

'So you have!' Alice laughed. 'Tell me. Come on. Confess. Better yet, show me.' She nodded towards Birdy who was turning his head this way and that, eyeing off both these extraordinary humans as if to say 'What on earth are they talking about?'

'Well,' Mr Brown began, 'to tell the truth, when I light the paraffin flame on my pokerwork burner it makes a powerful hiss – like steam being released, or gas from a broken pipe. Fred – I mean Birdy – learnt to mimic that to perfection.'

'Can I see?' Alice asked, fascinated. 'Can I hear?'

'Give me one minute,' Mr Brown agreed and, slipping back into his workroom, he reappeared with the pokerwork burner and a box of matches. He shook the bronze burner to check that it was filled with paraffin and pumped a valve on top to build up pressure. Once he released the valve, Alice heard the hiss of escaping gas. 'You see? You hear?' he asked gleefully, then, having struck a match, he applied its flame to the protruding nozzle and *Whoosh!* Now Mr Brown turned to the bird and gave a little bow, inviting its contribution. On cue, Birdy repeated the sound of the escaping gas – and as an encore, the *Whoosh!* of the ignited flame that followed.

'Goodness me!' Alice exclaimed. 'How smart is this bird?' but Birdy had experienced enough of human beings for one day and took off for the concealing shadows of the bush.

'Well,' Mr Brown said, 'I'm thinking you could use some breakfast since you were up so early. Keep your Vegemite sandwiches for lunch. What would you say to lovely hot toast – and I still have a bottle of Marcella's excellent fig jam.'

'Yes, please,' Alice said, 'and then I should go to school.'

CHAPTER NINE

THERE WAS SO MUCH TO TELL MR BROWN WHEN Alice visited – that was the trouble. Maybe they were both lonely. He lived alone and Alice was an only child. Besides, all her school friends lived miles away. So when she visited Mr Brown – every other day, as did Birdy – they would yabber on about all sorts of things such as flowering trees spotted in the bush and wildlife they had surprised down by the creek. And there was always the topic of Miss Kerr's love life and how Mr Solomon often dropped by on his way to the bank.

'He's manager now,' Miss Kerr told Alice, 'but I don't want to marry him just yet. Maybe one day, but not yet. My mother's in her eighties and needs me.' Alice never knew how to respond to that comment since it reminded her of how Mr Brown looked forward to her coming over – especially their tea and cake – and conversations about Birdy.

The truth was, Alice rarely got up early enough to see Birdy at Mr Brown's (or was that Birdy pretending to be Fred?). Besides, she was teaching the bird new sounds at her place, such as a teaspoon tapping against a china plate, the *rat-a-tat* of a tin drum she borrowed from Ron's room, the whine of a hand-wound siren Mr Solomon found in a drawer at the bank.

'I suppose it was intended for fire drills,' he explained to Alice and Miss Kerr one morning. 'But since we now have an electric alarm system, you can take it if you like. You might try it out on your lyrebird.'

Mr and Mrs Dorritt were not impressed by the hideous sound but Alice was delighted – and Birdy thoroughly enjoyed releasing the scream of the siren all over the bush.

The forest was sometimes drenched with two or three days' rain. The usually narrow creek ran wild in a muddy torrent, bursting its banks with clods of red earth; the great green fronds of the tree ferns drooped heavy and low, and the erratic paths of the forest animals were strewn with fallen branches. Bugs and beetles scrabbled through the chaos.

Alice loved the rain. She loved walking to school in her thick mackintosh, pretending she was safe and warm inside a shiny, black cocoon. She loved coming home too, especially when she could curl up beside her beautiful bedroom window, book in hand, and gaze into the dripping forest as the rain drummed on the galvanised-iron roof. She thought of Birdy, wondering where he might shelter in this downpour – or was he feasting on those scrabbling bugs and beetles?

During one especially wet weekend, when Alice's father brought her a mug of hot cocoa, she looked up from her book and said, 'Dad, why do people say that rain "drums" on the roof?'

Taken by surprise, her father answered, 'Goodness me. What an odd question. What brought that on?'

Alice shrugged. 'Can't really say, but Miss Kerr has been encouraging us to use the right word in the right place. So, maybe . . . ?' She shrugged again.

Her father put one hand to his ear and inclined his head towards the ceiling. 'Hmmm,' he muttered. 'Now I listen carefully, perhaps you're right. It's not really "drumming" on the roof, is it?'

Alice thought a moment. 'No. Drumming is "rat-a-tat-tat" or "boom-boom". This sound is more consistent. Sleepier, kind of. More like . . .'

'Humming!' her father exclaimed. 'When the downpour is consistent, I would say it's "humming".'

Alice laughed. 'I will tell Miss Kerr that. She'll say "Ernest Dorritt, that is an excellent answer. You may sit in the back row as a reward."'

'I would rather get back to my painting,' Ernie laughed.

'And since it's Saturday afternoon,' Alice declared, 'I'm going for a walk in the bush. I love it when the creek floods.'

'What about your hot cocoa?' he asked.

'Thanks for reminding me. I'll heat it up when I get back. It will taste all the better when I'm cold and wet,' Alice laughed and, pulling on her galoshes, she took her mac and rain hat from behind the back door, then slipped out into the dripping bush. 'There's nothing like walloping through the slop in your galoshes,' she called to the trees. 'Miss Kerr would like them words, I bet!' and off she walloped, the bugs and beetles scattering in all directions.

Since Alice had the time, after a long walk beside the raging creek, she stopped by Mr Brown's on the way home. With the rain still pouring down, he was sitting inside at his kitchen table, the log fire in his combustion stove roaring.

'Alice,' he said when he saw her at the door. 'Come in. It's warm in here and I've just made pumpkin scones. An old recipe that Marcella used to make. Take off your boots before you get mud everywhere.'

'They're not boots,' Alice giggled. 'They're galoshes. That's my expression for the day: mud-walloping galoshes, I call them.'

'There's no such word as "wallop",' he laughed. 'You made that up.'

'I know. And I like it. Miss Kerr said it's okay to make up words in poetry, and "mud-walloping galoshes" sounds like poetry to me,' Alice said as she took off her dripping mac.

'I won't argue with that. Now, take a scone off the griddle and pull up a chair. What have you got to tell me?'

'In spite of the rain, I've been for a walk in the forest,' she said, sitting down on a chair and, oddly enough, bending to slide something out of sight beneath it. 'I'm glad you don't have carpet,' she muttered as she straightened up.

'The weather's awful,' Mr Brown said, evidently confused by her secretive behaviour.

'I love walking in the rain,' Alice said. 'Besides, I had an adventure.'

Mr Brown put his cup down and leant forward, keen to hear.

Alice was only too happy to oblige, 'First, can I please butter one of those yummy-looking scones and pour a cup of tea? I'm being evil, I know, because Dad has a perfectly good mug of cocoa waiting for me at home. But who could resist?'

When she had made her tea, and buttered her scone to her satisfaction, Alice cleared her throat theatrically and began: 'I followed the creek for about two miles to the west of our place,' she said, waving her arm in the general direction, 'but then the path was blocked by a fallen tree. I guess the soil was so boggy that the weight of the rainwater in the foliage was too much for its roots to cope with and it just toppled over. There were bush orchids clinging to some of its branches and a bird's nest – an old one I think, because it was empty, thank goodness. Anyway, I climbed over the trunk and spotted a break in the bush that I hadn't noticed before. There's nothing like an adventure, I thought – so I pushed the branches aside and took a look. I saw another creek, running wild, just like ours. I'd never seen this one before. Maybe it only flows in heavy rain, or maybe it's usually only the tiniest tributary of our creek – who knows? – but it was new to me so I decided to explore. There was no clear path so I had to walk along the creek bank. That wasn't easy – there were more trees down and bushes toppled over and sticky mud everywhere . . . but I wanted to see where this creek was coming from. I mean, how dare the forest keep secrets from me? I was born here!'

'And you might have drowned here too,' Mr Brown observed, sipping his tea. 'Creeks in flood have notoriously dangerous banks. They can erode in lumps and sweep you away . . .'

'Oh, the banks *were* crumbling,' Alice declared, wide-eyed. 'Like you say, great lumps of clay were falling into the current but I did take care, Mr B. I did, honest. I saw so many orchids on the fallen trees and kept on going until I came to a sort of whirlpool of muddy water and sticks and stuff – maybe six or eight feet across and the water was swirling – and that seemed to be where this new creek was bubbling up from. Was it a spring, maybe? Or a stormwater outlet from the housing subdivision further upstream? What do you think?'

Mr Brown shook his head. 'I haven't been out that way in years,' he admitted. 'I really don't know.'

'Anyway, whatever it was, I'd found the source of the rushing creek and I didn't feel like climbing over and under any more tree trunks and getting scratched and bruised so I decided to go home. As I turned, I noticed something shiny sticking out of the muddy bank about three feet from where

I was standing. I thought, *That looks like a spearhead*, and laughed because that was silly – but when I turned to go again, something made me look back. *What is that?* I wondered, so I pulled my mac across my knees and knelt down.'

'You knelt down?' Mr Brown gasped. 'On that washed-out bank? Above a whirlpool? Alice!'

'I know, I know,' she sighed, shaking her head. 'Please don't tell Mum and Dad, but nothing ventured, nothing gained . . . Look, this is what I pulled out of the mud . . .' and reaching below her chair, she grasped the object she had secreted there and held it out.

Mr Brown gasped again.

'Do you have any newspaper?' she asked. 'It's still pretty muddy and I don't want to dirty your tablecloth.'

'I've got last Sunday's paper. We can use that.'

Alice waited until he'd spread the paper over the tablecloth then very carefully placed the object on its wrinkled surface, wiping the mud off her hands on the edge of the paper. 'I don't know what it is,' she said. 'It's got marks on it. That's why I stopped by to ask you.'

Mr Brown leant forward, his fingers outstretched.

'As I said, at first I thought it was a spearhead. It's that shape, isn't it? But when I pulled it out of the mud and turned it over, I saw that it was a piece of stone.'

'It could always be a stone spearhead. Flint, at least . . .' he said.

Alice nodded. 'That's true, but as I turned it in my hand a dollop of mud dropped off . . .'

'A "dollop"?' He raised his eyebrows at this new word. 'I thought mud came in "wallops". That's what you said, "Mud-walloping galoshes".'

'You're funny, Mr B,' Alice giggled. '"Wallop" is a verb. It's what a person does when they muck about in mud. It's a "doing word". "Dollop" is a noun. It's a "thing": a lump of mud in this case.'

Mr Brown rolled his eyes, evidently trying to keep up with this walking, talking lexicon.

'And when the mud dropped off, I saw these marks on the surface. See? They're really fine, like fibrous roots . . .' She used her index finger to point out what she meant. 'I tell you what, I should rinse it off under running water. Then we'll be able to see better. Okay?'

'Just hold it out in the rain,' Mr Brown said, so Alice picked up the stone and, holding it in the palm of her hand, took it out onto the back verandah where she leant out and washed it beneath the overflowing guttering on the roof.

'There,' she said, triumphantly placing it back on the paper.

Mr Brown folded the edges of the newspaper over and patted the surface of the object dry. 'That's better,' he said. 'Now we can decide what on earth it is.'

The stone was a deep grey-green, about nine inches long, pointed at both ends, and three inches at its widest across the middle. The delicate root-like impressions fanned out to cover the surface from a deeper groove running from tip to tip.

'It doesn't appear to be made by a human being,' Mr Brown observed. 'Those grooves are not what I would call *intaglio*.'

It was Alice's turn to raise her eyebrows. '"Intaglio"?' she repeated. 'Now you're making words up.'

'No. That's an Italian word meaning "engraved". The grooves are too organic for human manufacture – or design.' He sat back and scratched his chin. 'Alice,' he said, 'I believe you have found a fossil.'

Alice was delighted. 'So, it's not just any old rock or a bit of broken pipe washed down from the housing development in the flood? It's really old, do you think?'

'Old? It's old all right! All fossils are very old, but how old – from what period – I have no idea.'

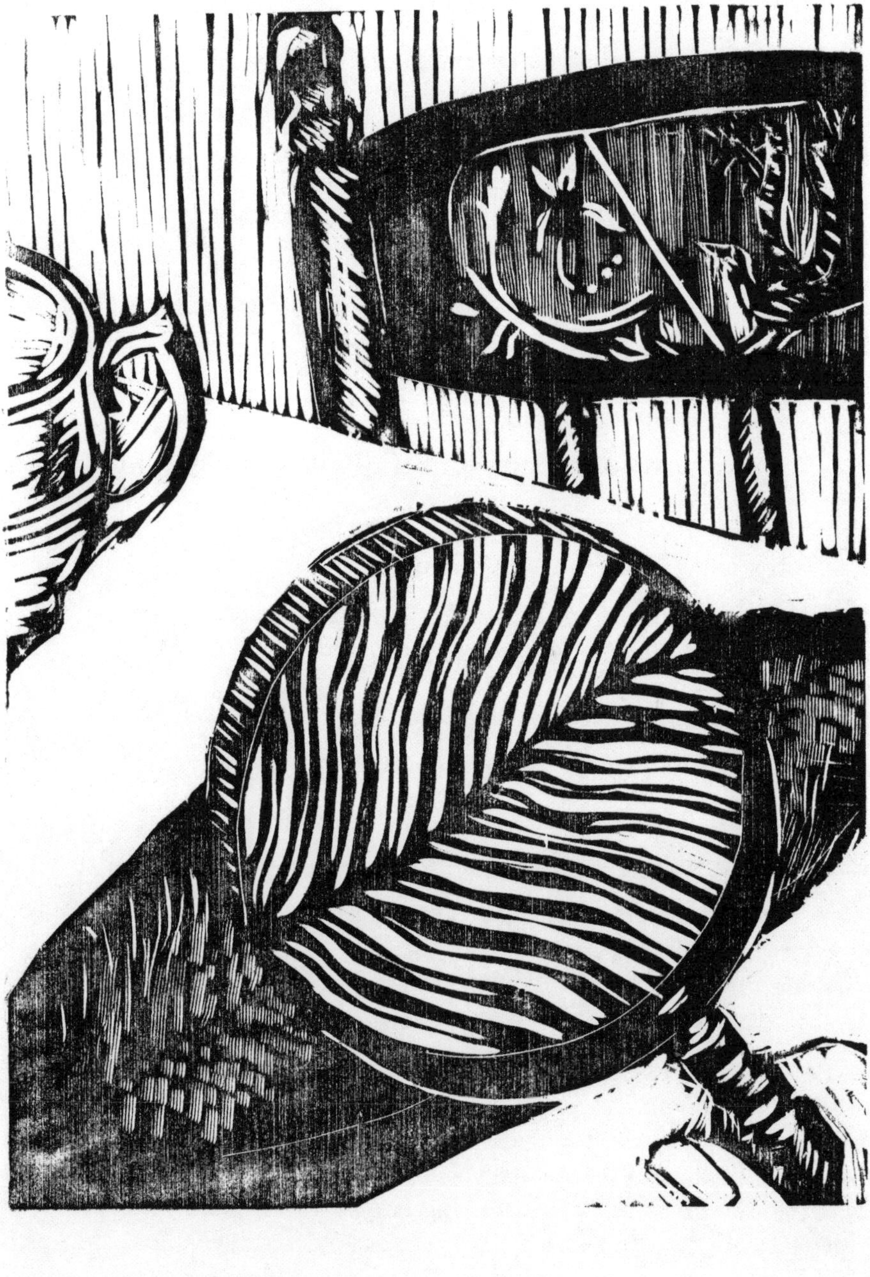

'And what's that on it, do you think? Roots? Fossilised roots?'

Mr Brown rubbed the surface of the fossil reverently. 'Could be roots,' he mused. 'Or it could be a fern. A fern pressed in mud a billion years ago. Or a leaf? A lovely thing. Remarkable really. But what it is, exactly, who knows?'

'But it's rare, you think?'

'I'm no expert, but I'd say so, though I wonder . . .'

'What? You wonder what?'

'If there were more?'

'In the bank of the whirlpool?'

'Or that creek that you discovered.'

Alice shook her head. 'It was too dangerous to look any further. And the rain was pouring down . . .'

'I wonder,' Mr Brown said again, this time more to himself. 'Where was this creek that you found?'

Alice explained as best she could where she had deviated from the track along the main creek and Mr Brown nodded, taking it all in. 'It's not hard,' she said, 'I just followed the main creek until a fallen tree blocked my way. The forest has changed, hasn't it?' She looked down at the fossil. 'And that's sad.'

Mr Brown lifted his head to meet her gaze. 'One day we will all have to let nature have its way,' he said. 'Like those trees that fell, none of us can live forever.'

'I should go,' Alice said. 'Mum and Dad will be worried. And Dad did make me cocoa. It will be stone cold by now. Goodbye Mr B, and thanks for explaining all of that to me. I'll fetch my mac – and my galoshes – then wallop on home.'

But as she fussed with the sticky, wet mac, she forgot to take the fossil – so suddenly exposed to accounts of everyday life after millions of years.

When Alice left, walloping off into the mud, Cyril picked up the fossil, turning it carefully in his fingers as he examined it more closely. With a few huffs and puffs, he fetched a magnifying glass from his workroom, and sat outside under the cover of the back verandah roof to examine the discovery in better light.

'Interesting . . .' he muttered. 'Very interesting!' Without further thought he took off his red corduroy slippers (spotting the holes in the green woollen socks beneath) and pulled on his bushwalking boots. 'Rain or no rain. Mud or no mud, it's time to follow that creek,' he said to no one, heading down the gully behind his house. Once he reached the torrent that was usually the trickle they called 'the creek', he followed its course to the west, constantly forced to leave the boggy track where heavy vegetation blocked his path. But for all of his diversions, he had a pretty good idea where he was going. Years before, with young Ronald at his side, Cyril remembered stumbling upon a tiny creek that joined the one he was following – it had been no more than a trickle. That was the reason he'd questioned Alice about where she found the fossil, although back then – preoccupied as he was with

Ronald – he hadn't followed the new-found creek. His son was very young at the time and whingeing to go home. Ronald had never cared for the bush. In the present, Cyril tramped on, ducking under fallen branches and taking care not to lose his boots in patches of oozy, khaki-coloured mud.

After hours of walking (Cyril had abandoned wearing a watch as he grew older), his long-term memory – maybe his intuition – told him that he was near the place that Alice spoke of and he began peering into the scrub to his right. As he did, he heard wild water rumbling and gurgling and pushed aside the bushes. Clambering through, he exclaimed, 'Gotcha!' as another creek came into view – but the moment he saw the lumps of clay slipping from the bank, he stopped, his hand to his mouth.

'My goodness,' he muttered, 'this is dangerous,' and he clutched a fallen branch to ensure that he didn't plunge headlong into the surging water. 'Alice,' he said to himself, 'you were foolish – or very brave – I'm not sure which.'

Grabbing at overhanging branches as he went, he set out to follow the course of the new creek. 'I'm not liking this,' he said, 'I'm getting old and who would help me if I fell in . . . ?' Still the water rushed by, filled with logs and sheets of galvanised iron and fence posts entangled with barbed wire, and still the lumps of clay fell from the bank, dangerously undercutting the narrow path that ran alongside. Yet, as luck would have it, just as Cyril was thinking of turning back, he spotted the whirlpool Alice had so clearly described.

The threat of erosion collapsing the bank beneath his feet as he looked down was so great that he stretched both arms back to grip the bushes behind but – like a bird staring wide-eyed into the jaws of an advancing cat – he could not resist taking a closer look. 'Oh dear!' he declared. 'It's a maelstrom. Alice! Alice! Alice . . .' and then, just as the girl had done, he spotted something shiny protruding from the clay bank maybe eighteen inches below his feet. Something pointy, like a spearhead.

'Another one,' he gasped and, with one hand still gripping a branch, he dropped to his knees in the mud. 'I think I can get it,' he grunted. 'I have to . . .' and he did! But no sooner had he put the stone on the ground beside him and got to his feet than he saw another poking enticingly from the crumbling bank. Cyril knew that if he didn't retrieve that stone it would be swept away in moments.

'I can't have that happening,' he said. 'I can't . . .' and risking his life again, he knelt.

Once more, he reached.

Far down.

Once more, he grasped and retrieved.

'No more,' he said when he had two shining rocks lying in the mud at his feet. 'No more or there will be nobody to carry them home,' and satisfied with his afternoon's work, he gathered up his muddy find and started the journey home – though he chose not to wallop. He didn't have the energy.

CHAPTER TEN

The following Monday, Cyril Brown took the dray into town. He didn't do this very often, but he needed groceries and intended to drop off his latest pokerwork creation (a teapot stand featuring the rare mountain-bird orchid) – although the real reason was that he wanted to see the postmaster, Harry Shields. Harry and Cyril had been mates since they worked as posties in Lilydale and, from time to time, they'd catch up to sink a beer (or two) at the local pub. On this visit, however, the beer would have to wait – even though it was Harry's shout – since Cyril needed Harry's advice.

'Been busy, Cyril?' Harry asked when they sat at the bar of the Farmer's Friend. 'Retirement must be hell.'

'Flat out like a lizard drinking,' Cyril laughed. 'Unlike some who only pretend to be gainfully employed.'

'I've never worked so hard in my whole life,' Harry protested. 'Except when I rode my bike up and down those hills outside Lilydale delivering mail.'

'Who can forget?' Cyril replied. 'But Harry, I've got something to tell you – and I need your advice.'

'Shoot,' Harry encouraged.

Cyril recounted Alice's story of her discovery of the fossil and how he had trekked through the forest to find two more with the same markings. He showed Harry one of the stones he had found.

Harry studied the rock carefully. Declining another beer (he had to return to work), he said, 'Cyril, my old mate, if you were asking about pokerwork, I could help – you know that I'm way better at it than you – but I know nothing about prehistoric fossils. Why are you asking me?'

The bartender slid a beer in Cyril's direction. 'I'm allowed,' Cyril said with a nod. 'I'm retired, remember? Harry, I'm asking you because you know stuff about people who know stuff . . .'

'What does that mean?' Harry laughed. 'You're getting old, mate.'

'Listen, Harry, I'm asking for your advice as postmaster. I'm asking the advice of the man who sees mail addressed to experts in every profession: doctors, lawyers, architects, agriculturalists . . . You name it.'

'So? I don't *know* them. I just process the mail addressed to them.'

Cyril sighed. 'I know that you don't know them personally, but at least you know the names of some of the career experts and what they specialise in. Don't you?'

Harry gave that some thought. 'Yes . . .' he admitted. 'I see their names on envelopes. So?'

'What sort of person should I contact to tell them about these fossils we found – if that's what they are?'

'Well,' Harry said, 'I once saw an envelope addressed to a Dr Dino of Fossilised Flats. Could he help?'

'I don't believe you,' Cyril scoffed. 'And your bad jokes are getting worser.'

'There's no such word as "worser",' Harry protested.

'And there's no such person as Dr Dino. Come on, think. Who should I contact?'

They were silent for a minute then Harry said, 'I could find the address of the National Museum of Victoria. They must have an expert in fossils working there.'

'Yeah?'

'What I'm saying is that you could send one of your rocks – whatever they are – to the museum in the city. They might chuck it away but you would always have a couple left to use as paperweights.'

'Ha, ha! Not funny. But thanks, Harry. I'll do that as soon as you get me the address of the museum. Okay?'

'That's part of my job, mate,' Harry said, getting to his feet. 'Come on, old man, you don't want to be falling down drunk.'

As Alice sauntered along the forest trail returning from school some weeks later, she heard voices coming from Mr Brown's house. *That's odd*, she thought, and being a stickybeak (though she justified her intrusion by pretending that she was acting in Mr Brown's best interests), she turned down the path towards his house.

Imagine her astonishment when she saw Mr Brown sitting on his front verandah with a very attractive young woman whose hair was the same colour as her own. 'Sorry to interrupt,' Alice called from the base of the stairs, 'but I thought you might need my help, Mr B.'

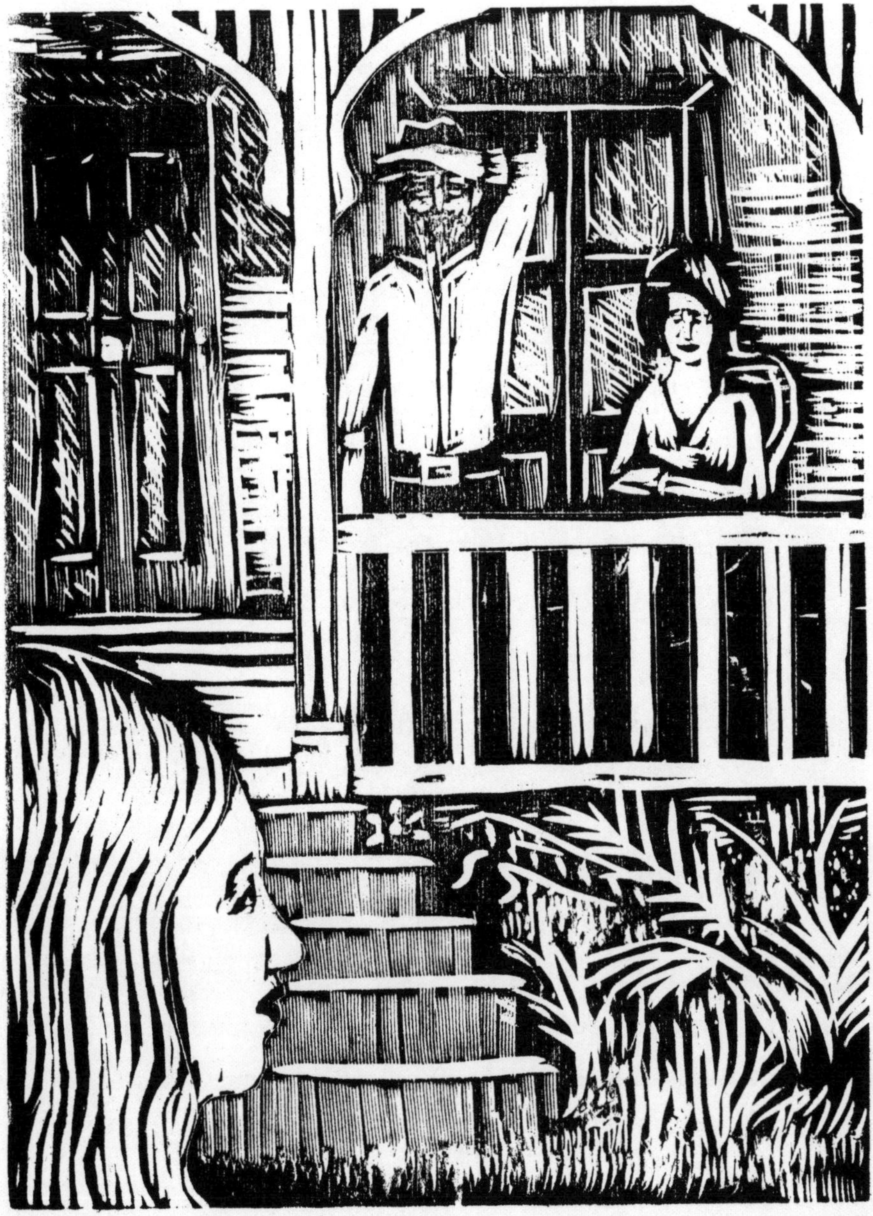

Cyril Brown laughed. 'I'm fine, thanks Alice. This is Grace Nicholas. She's from the National Museum of Victoria. Did I get that right, Grace?'

'You did very well, Mr Brown,' Grace said.

Alice was delighted. *How beautiful is this girl – this woman?* Alice thought. *Her skin is perfect. And her teeth. And even though her hair is the same colour as mine, it looks good. And she must be very smart if she works at the museum.* 'What kind of work do you do, if I may ask?'

'I have a degree in Science, majoring in Biology,' Grace answered. 'I did my Honours thesis researching endangered wildlife. I'm employed by the museum as a naturalist to keep tabs on species on the brink of extinction.'

Confused, Alice looked to Mr Brown.

'Acting on my friend Harry Shields' advice,' Mr Brown said '– Alice, you know Harry Shields from the post office in town? – I sent that rock we found to the museum and it ended up on Grace's desk.'

Astonished, Alice looked from one to the other. '*My* rock?' she asked in disbelief. 'You sent my fossil to the museum? How come?'

'No, not your rock, Alice; it's still here safe and sound . . .'

Mr Brown invited Alice onto the verandah and patted the chair beside him. 'I've been meaning to tell you,' he explained when she was seated. 'After you showed me the fossil, I remembered that I had seen that creek you discovered years ago – when my boy Ronald was knee-high to a grasshopper – so I went back and found it again. And Alice, you'll be pleased to know that I found two more stones with the same marks on them. Almost identical. Only then did I begin to appreciate the significance of your find: that the fossil *you* found, and the fossils *I* found could be from a site of prehistoric significance. So, like I said, I sent one of the rocks to the museum to find out what they might make of it . . .'

'That's true,' Grace said. 'And my boss, Dr Ingram, who's a palaeontologist – sorry, that's a specialist in fossils – confirmed that it was a fossil of some description and has sent me to see what I think about further investigating the site.'

Disappointed to have missed out on these negotiations, Alice looked down and sighed.

'Sorry, Alice,' Mr Brown offered. 'But you go to school most days and I have time to do these things. Besides, thankfully I'm still healthy enough to get about by myself.'

'You're right,' Alice agreed. 'I'm sorry too. I was being selfish. So, Grace, what do you think about what we found?'

Grace smiled. '"Found" is an interesting word,' she said. 'That's like saying Captain Cook "found" the Australian continent when he didn't, considering neither place – the creek bank nor Australia – was ever lost. In fact, having been to the site with Cyril this morning and seen the sedimentary strata of the rock exposed by the storm,

I'd say there's a strong possibility that there are more fossils buried there. But I'm no expert and I don't know exactly what sort of fossils they are. I'm just a junior researcher. Dr Ingram wanted me to see if the location was worthy of further study and I believe that it is.'

'You do? Really?'

'I do. I intend to write a report detailing what we've seen; I've taken photos,' – she indicated a canvas tote bag at her feet – 'and I'm certain that the museum will send out a team to investigate. By the way, Cyril, do many people come by here – like bushwalkers or sightseers?'

'Virtually no one,' he assured her. 'In fact, other than Alice, I don't think anyone would have been out that way since I was there with my son – and that was years ago.'

'Good,' Grace said, 'but as a precaution, I'm going to recommend that a team comes in to put up signs to cordon off that pool as soon as possible.

We don't want any stickybeaks mooching about – and certainly no souvenir hunters.'

'But what sort of fossil might it be?' Alice asked. 'I mean, what might make it special?'

'If my first impression is right,' Grace said, 'this particular fossil could be very rare. Very rare indeed!' And she gave Mr Brown a mysterious wink.

'Mr B!' Alice cried. 'What's going on here? What's the secret? Come on.'

'Well . . .' Now it was Cyril's turn to wink at Grace, who giggled.

'You're not being fair,' Alice said. 'After all, I'm the one who found it. Mr B, you just followed my track, didn't you? Now tell me.'

'Well . . .' he began again, 'after you'd gone home that rainy Saturday, I sat on the verandah and looked at your find under my magnifying glass – and what I saw got me thinking.'

'Yes, yes. Go on,' Alice encouraged.

'So, I went back up the creek and found two more specimens . . .'

'We all know that, Mr B. Get to the point. Come on.'

Cyril raised his hand, seeking silence. 'The next Monday I went into town to see my old friend Harry Shields, the postmaster.'

'I know! And I know who the postmaster is. Stop teasing, please!'

'After Harry had taken a close look at this silly old rock – I'm joking, I'm joking – he said, "I know nothing about fossils, but having given this rock the once-over, Cyril" – that's my Christian name, in case you didn't know, Miss Impatience – "I don't think this is the fossil of a leaf or a fern. Not the fossil of a plant, that is. I'm wondering if Alice has gone and found herself the fossil of a *feather*!"'

Alice clapped her hand to her mouth.

'And I think it might be possible he's right,' Grace said.

'No!' Alice declared. 'A feather?'

'And no fossilised feather has ever been found in Australia,' Grace added with delight.

'Really?' Alice could hardly believe it.

'Really and truly,' Grace replied, crossing her heart. 'In fact, there are very few examples of fossilised feathers in the whole world.'

'Tell me more,' Alice begged.

'I'm no expert on palaeontology,' Grace began, 'but so far as I can remember from my student days, back in the 1860s the single fossilised feather of an archaeopteryx was found in a limestone quarry in Germany.'

'A what?' Alice gasped.

'An archaeopteryx,' Grace said, laughing.

'What sort of word is that? We're learning about new words at school.'

'The word "archaeopteryx" means "ancient wing" in Latin. I think. The archaeopteryx was a sort of flying dinosaur.'

'A "sort of flying dinosaur"? What does that mean? Was it a bird or a dinosaur? I thought dinosaurs were reptiles.'

Grace hesitated, 'There's still some debate among scientists on that issue.'

'Haven't they decided yet?'

'Some say one thing, some another.'

'Even now? After all these years?'

'Even now. And it gets more complicated. In 1861 it was revealed that the complete fossilised skeleton of an archaeopteryx had been discovered. Some claimed this was a fake, that someone had combined other ancient fossils to make a false skeleton. I don't know the full story, but the British palaeontologist Richard Owen managed to acquire this fossil – fake or genuine – for the British Natural History Museum. Whatever it was they'd found, the great scientist Thomas Huxley said that the feathered creature was "dinosaur-like". I can't explain that any better than he did. I'm not an expert in that field. What I *do* know is that there's still a great deal of research to be done on early life forms and that very few feathers have been found in fossils. Certainly, none in Australia, so . . .'

Alice's mind was racing. 'So, this could be a brand new discovery? I could go to university and study this, couldn't I?'

'You certainly could. I only read a bit about these issues when I was at university, before I decided to give my full attention to studying endangered Australian animals and I couldn't keep up with all the new research into palaeontology. Still, I love the research I do at the moment and it sounds like you would too. Palaeontology is all about what has come before but I am studying what is happening now – it feels like you're going where nobody has been before. It's really exciting.'

'So, if what we found really are fossilised feathers, they would be super important to science and understanding our past. Like, finding out if there is a connection between birds and reptiles, right?'

'Quite right. As I said, that issue is still being researched. At this time, we really don't know.'

Alice beamed. 'I could be the first woman – maybe the first person – to make that link. Couldn't I?'

'With your enquiring mind,' Cyril said, 'I'm sure you would be a great asset to science. You should consider that, Alice.'

Alice looked away, wondering: *Me! Imagine going to university to study fossils. Or endangered animals. Maybe to study birds like lyrebirds. That could be me. I'd have to leave the forest but I'd come back to care for lyrebird chicks and Mum and Dad would be so proud. And Mr Brown.* As she glanced at her friend, another thought crossed her mind: Mr Brown was far from young. He couldn't live forever. He could die while she was away – if she went away – or at any time. As was the case for all living things.

Naturally.

As she mused, Mr Brown got to his feet. 'There's still some of that rich dark fruit cake that Alice's mother sent over. What do you say, Grace?'

Grace glanced at her wristwatch. 'My train isn't due until seven,' she said. 'So yes please, I'd love some cake. And a cup of tea.'

'Nothing for me,' Alice said. 'I've got heaps of homework. I'm in year eight now, Grace, and if I want to make anything of myself, I need to get a good result in my exams next month – especially since my mum and dad want me to be a boarder at a high school that's miles away. Exam time. Do you remember that time of year?'

'I certainly do,' Grace agreed. 'But now I'm glad that I studied, and I hope that you do the same. I love my job.'

'Bye, Grace,' Alice said. 'Bye, Mr B.' She walked home briskly, her head spinning with a thousand thoughts of an uncertain future.

CHAPTER ELEVEN

DAWDLING HOME FROM SCHOOL SOME WEEKS later, Alice spotted a horse and dray tethered to a tree at the entrance to the track leading to Mr Brown's house. She stroked the horse's velvety nose then stood on tiptoe to see what was stacked on the dray. *Interesting,* she thought, spotting shovels and trowels and sieves. *Is someone thinking of doing some gardening? That's odd. The bush needs no help* . . . Snoop that she was, she turned down the track to ask Mr Brown.

Sure enough, she found him dozing on his front verandah. 'Alice,' he declared. 'You've missed all the excitement. The museum people came to investigate the fossil site so we sat and talked . . .' he indicated the teacups on a pokerwork tray, 'but now they've gone off up the creek to have a look.'

'How long will they be here?' she asked.

He shrugged. 'There were three men and a woman: Dr Ingram, Grace's boss at the museum, was one of them. I missed the woman's name but it wasn't Grace, she didn't come. Sorry.'

'I'm sorry too. I would have loved to see her again,' Alice sighed. 'But the others have to come back for their horse and dray, don't they?'

'They're staying at the hotel in town tonight. Don't worry, they'll be back here before dark.'

Alice nodded, preparing to leave, but on the instant, she turned, beaming; 'Mr B,' she said, 'tomorrow is our school's athletics day. I always come last – and I hate coming last at anything – especially in some stupid race. How about I take a day off, I'll ask Mum to make a thermos flask of tea and some sandwiches, and we go up the creek to see what they're doing?'

Mr Brown was delighted. 'Better yet,' he said, 'tomorrow's Birdy's day to visit me, right? How about you come even earlier to see him, and then we can go – with a flask and lunch, of course.'

'And some cake,' Alice laughed, also delighted.

Early next morning Alice was pleased to see the horse and dray tethered at the base of Mr Brown's front steps. So, they've left already, she thought, and bounded up to meet Mr Brown.

Birdy graciously accepted the delicious worms Alice offered on the verandah outside Mr Brown's workroom. 'Birdy's not as picky as he used to be,' she observed. 'Once upon a time he wouldn't touch those slimy brown worms but now he eats them first.'

'That reminds me of Ronald,' Mr Brown laughed. 'He'd never eat pumpkin, not even Marcella's pumpkin scones, but once he finally tried it, he loved it.'

'I like pumpkin,' Alice admitted. 'Dad says that's where my red hair came from. Okay, enough chitchat. Birdy's finished so we can go. See? I've got our goodies in my schoolbag . . .' She indicated the smart leather satchel her mother had made for her. 'If I wear this over my shoulders, I'll have my arms free to stop me falling into the creek.'

The track beside the creek was now much more defined, having been trampled by the museum investigators.

'It's a shame,' Cyril said. 'I know this has to be done, and we're just as bad but the bush can only take so much traffic.'

Alice was following close behind. 'But you built your house here,' she pointed out. 'And so did my parents. That's worse.'

'True,' he agreed. 'Very true. Though we were younger and stupider. Well, not stupid really, but certainly ignorant. Marcella and I had no idea of the impact we would have on the scrub. The track in front of our house was made to haul timber out last century and when we built, we just accepted that was how things were done. As I say, we were ignorant. After we'd moved in, it didn't take us long to notice that wildlife which had once been plentiful stopped showing up.'

'What sort of wildlife?'

'Well, the growling grass frog for a start.'

'The what?'

'A frog with a growly kind of croak.'

'Really?'

Mr Brown turned. 'I'm not joking. They were huge – dark green and about four inches long. They used to flop onto the verandah to squat in patches of sun. I hardly see them now.'

'I've never seen one,' Alice sighed.

'They used to come up from the creek. This creek was wider then. Much wider. Its main course has been diverted to irrigate farms and for the housing development – so called – nearer to town. The tadpoles were great fat things. Ronald used to love watching them. Gone now. All gone.'

'Did you tell Grace about the frogs?'

'Grace knew about them,' he said. 'Sadly, she reminded *me* . . .'

After tramping for ages, they saw a network of ropes looped from tree to tree with cardboard signs attached, saying, 'KEEP OUT'.

'We're there,' Cyril said.

Alice hardly recognised the spot. The whirlpool was nothing more than a puddle – its sides no longer lined with mud falling into the water in great lumps; rather they were more like solidified clay, riddled with cracks and fissures as they dried out after the heavy rain from the storm some weeks before. In the bottom of this hole were three men, two young men scraping the sides, one older man on his knees, carefully probing at the repository of drying mud at the bottom. No sooner did they hear Mr Brown's voice than the man at the bottom of the pit raised his head and called, 'I'm sorry. We're working here. Please keep back.'

The speaker was a thin, grey-haired gent in his fifties. He wore round, gold-framed glasses, grey overalls, black gloves made of cloth, and carried a trowel.

'Dr Ingram, it's me, Cyril Brown, and Alice, who found the place.'

'Oh, I know who you are, Cyril – and many thanks for your sharp observation in finding the fossil, Alice. I don't mean to be rude, but this is now the site of a serious investigation. You must excuse us if we don't stop.'

Alice stood back, afraid of being a nuisance.

'I'm sorry,' Dr Ingram continued, 'but if you're happy to watch from up there, that's okay.'

'We understand,' Mr Brown nodded. 'We're just stickybeaking. You go on.' Finding a convenient log not far back from the rope line, he spread out his handkerchief for Alice to sit on.

'I can stand,' Alice protested, but gentleman that he was, Mr Brown insisted.

The men continued to scrape the walls and floor of the pit, communicating with each other in low tones, sometimes stopping to show something they had unearthed to one another. It seemed to Alice that, if they agreed that what they had found was worthwhile, that item was placed carefully in a manila envelope, which was sealed and labelled. When bagged and tagged, each object was placed in a pine box – the size of a fruit box – lined with straw. Some objects that appeared too big for envelopes were placed directly into the box. Once the object was packed away, its original location was marked on a site map pinned to a wooden clipboard that dangled from a string hanging over the side of the pit.

'I wish I knew what they were finding,' Alice whispered to Mr Brown. 'I wish I could get down there and help.'

Mr Brown smiled. 'I'm sure they know what they're doing,' he reassured her.

'You said there was a woman,' Alice said, looking around. 'Where's she?'

Mr Brown nodded towards their left. At first Alice could see nothing, then she caught the flash of metal in a gap among the ferns on the far side of the pit. To her delight, she saw a camera mounted on a tripod and a young woman in khaki trousers bending over it, evidently adjusting a lens.

'She's outside of the rope,' Alice whispered. 'I'm going around. Okay?'

'I don't think I could stop you,' Mr Brown laughed and Alice was gone.

In a matter of minutes, Alice presented herself beside the camera, face flushed and eyes wide with excitement. 'Hello,' she said. 'I'm Alice Dorritt. I live near here and I found this place . . .' Then she remembered. 'Sorry, Grace from the museum said that I shouldn't say "found" because the site was never lost.' Since all of this was said in one breath and having stumbled and bumbled through the

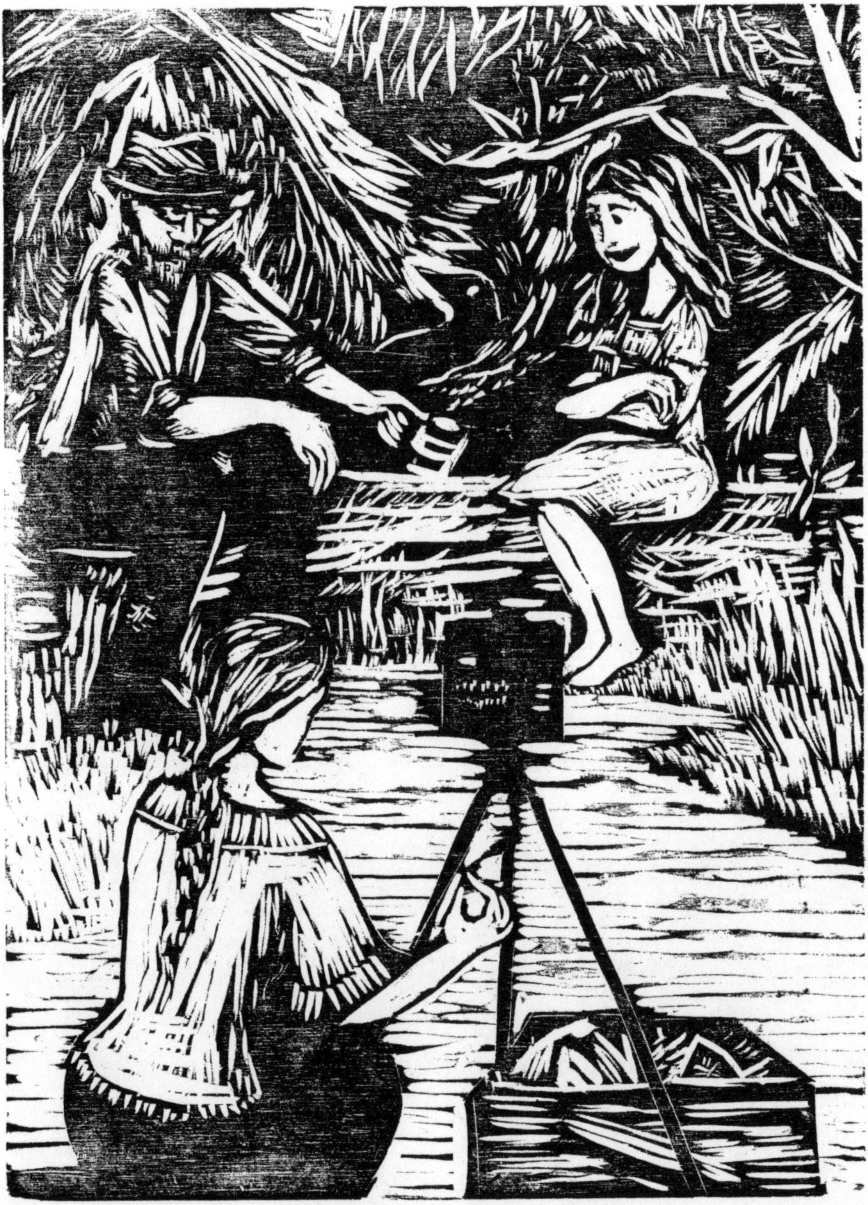

scrub in such a rush, Alice's cheeks were flushed and her hair mad with twigs and leaves.

'Oh!' declared the woman, 'I thought you were some native animal bursting out on me. I'm Sheila Kavanagh. So, you know Grace?'

Now Alice was embarrassed. 'Sorry,' she said, brushing down her dress. 'I didn't mean to frighten you. Yes, Grace came by a few weeks ago. She was sent to follow up on a letter that Mr Brown over there sent to the museum about this place.'

'Okay,' Sheila laughed, 'but believe me, it would take more than you to frighten me. I've photographed the biggest and the wildest.'

'Such as?' Alice blurted out. 'Gorillas?'

Sheila laughed again. 'Gorillas might be big but they aren't really wild. They're shy. Judging by the way you came up to me, you're not shy either, are you?'

'I am with boys,' Alice admitted, lowering her eyes. 'A bit. I'm an only child, see. I mean, I don't have any brothers. So, maybe . . .'

'Alice, you don't have to justify yourself to me. I work with boys – well, men, I suppose you'd call them – almost every day . . .' She took her hand from the camera and made a sweep of the male workers beyond the rope. 'Give me gorillas any day. But don't tell Dr Ingram I said that.'

'I promise,' Alice giggled. 'But have you really worked with gorillas? In Africa?'

'In London Zoo,' Sheila explained. 'Poor things. They were so unhappy, being confined. I photographed them for *National Geographic*. I did what they called a "photo essay" on zoos. But now I'm here, really in the wild, and doing what I love.'

'Do you work for the museum?'

'No. I'm my own boss. People like Grace and Dr Ingram who want photographs taken of wildlife – or wild places – contact me and ask me to do such and such. I've got the experience and the equipment.' She indicated her camera. 'It's a great life.'

'What's your job here today?' Alice asked.

Beaming, she said, 'My job is to photograph the site as it was – undisturbed, so to speak – I did that as soon as we arrived. Now I'm taking shots of the actual field work in progress, then close-ups of the excavated area. I'll get the smaller stuff that they've bagged back in the museum. You follow?'

'Yes, I do,' Alice said, 'but will you have time to eat? That's my neighbour, Mr Brown, over there. I've brought plenty of sandwiches and a thermos of tea. Would you like to join us?'

'I met Mr Brown,' Sheila said. 'Nice man. Just give me a few minutes to finish these long shots and I'll be right over.'

'Okay,' Alice said, but Sheila already had her eye to the camera.

'You know, Mr B,' Alice began as she unpacked the lunch, 'there are just so many interesting careers a girl can have these days.'

He was putting the sandwiches out on serviettes that Mrs Dorritt had so kindly provided. 'I'm listening . . .' he said.

'Well, I really liked the idea of the work that Grace was doing, researching animals in danger of extinction, but now that I've met Sheila and seen what she does, I love that too.'

'You mean Sheila the photographer?' he asked.

Alice bit the corner off a ham sandwich. 'She's a pretty tough lady who's seen a lot, I'd say. And she's certainly not keen on men.'

'What's her surname? Do you know?'

'Kavanagh,' Alice said. 'Her full name is Sheila Kavanagh. And we had better leave some sandwiches because I asked her over for lunch.'

'Sheila Kavanagh, eh?' Mr Brown mused. 'I thought I detected the remnants of an Irish brogue. And yes, the Irish have learnt to be tough. In fact, they've had to be tough to survive.' As he spoke, Sheila appeared before them.

'Alice,' she said, smiling down at them. 'Mr Brown, we meet again. Tell me, since you're locals, have you ever seen any lyrebirds around here? I'm keen to get a photo of one if I can.' Then seeing them cast sidelong glances at each other, she demanded, 'What's so funny? Did I miss something?'

When they'd eaten, Sheila returned to her work while Grace and Mr Brown watched the men excavating in the pit with growing fascination.

'They're so careful,' Alice observed. 'They don't look like gorillas to me.'

'Gorillas?' Mr Brown queried. 'What gorillas?'

Alice blushed. 'Nothing,' she said. 'Forget it.'

'And they're so serious,' Mr Brown said, having no idea what Alice had meant. 'You see that they never appear to make jokes. They're paying complete attention to whatever they find. Very serious indeed.'

Later in the afternoon, the young men scrambled out of the pit and hauled Dr Ingram out after them. They stood in a circle, talking for about ten minutes then, while the other two clambered down again, Dr Ingram dusted himself off and walked over to Alice and Mr Brown.

'No doubt you're wondering what we've found,' he said.

'Can you tell us?' Alice asked.

Dr Ingram rubbed his chin. 'We found three or four more very good fossil samples,' he said. 'Very good.'

'But are they fossils of ferns, or leaves, or *feathers*?' Alice blurted out.

Now, for the first time, the scientist smiled. 'Feathers?' he said. 'What a dream that would be. Sorry Alice, I doubt that they're feathers – but I'm not saying they're not . . .'

'Oh,' Alice couldn't help herself from sounding disappointed. 'I so wanted . . .'

'And so did I! So do I! You need to understand that all scientific discovery is an exacting process, demanding examination and proof. Our samples need to be sent away for further examination before any definitive answer can be given. That could take months, even years. Are you happy with that?'

'Very happy,' Alice conceded. 'But I will be even happier when you tell me that what you've found are the fossils of lyrebird feathers. Could they be? Do you think?'

Dr Ingram gave Mr Brown a knowing look. 'We can always hope,' he answered. 'Lyrebirds are among the most intelligent creatures. They must have walked this earth – and flown these heavens – for millions of years. There's a chance that you may be right. We can but hope. So, thank you for all your help. It's been wonderful to be here. Now I must get back to packing what we've found for the museum.'

As he left, Alice turned to Mr Brown. 'So they could be lyrebird feathers, couldn't they?' she asked.

Mr Brown smiled. 'He didn't say "no",' he said. 'But the history of the lyrebird population in Australia is something you could research when you're a scientist yourself.'

On hearing this, Alice stood tall. 'Or a nature photographer,' she laughed, giving Sheila the thumbs-up across the pit.

CHAPTER TWELVE

WHAT MR BROWN TOLD ALICE ABOUT THE disappearing growling frogs made a lasting impression on the girl, as did meeting Grace and Sheila. As a result, she walked a lot, and thought a lot, growing more and more keen to gain a university degree that would qualify her to help or research and document wildlife under threat. But for all of her hopes and dreams of a career, she was still wary of leaving the forest. Then again, she couldn't agree with many of the girls in her class who were thinking of leaving school altogether to become hairdressers or dressmakers or marrying and becoming mothers. Alice couldn't imagine herself being any of those. When the museum team had left the forest, she devoted herself to schoolwork, determined to score good results and, hopefully, gain a scholarship to a respected boarding school – but she was also well aware of the drawbacks if she made it: she would pine for her parents, Mr Brown, the forest and, of course, her beloved Birdy.

'Birdy,' she called when he came tapping at her window, 'I might be going away soon. Not forever. I'll be back for the holidays but if I'm going to get an education so that I can care for birds and animals, I will have to leave. You're a bird, not a human – though you're more talented than most of us – so one day you might also need protection. Besides, I'm sure you would've left me. You would. Like Mr Solomon, you'd go looking for a mate. It's only natural. We all come and go, you know, one way or another. Sorry, Birdy, but nothing lasts forever – that's what Mum and Dad say.'

After this unexpected sermon, Birdy stared at Alice long and hard. 'Sorry,' she said, 'I guess you knew all of that anyway, Mr Smarty Feathers.' Birdy remained unmoved until, with a knowing blink, he resumed his wriggling breakfast.

One afternoon in her final year, as Alice gathered her books in preparation for her long walk home, Miss Kerr asked her to stay back a moment. 'Alice,' her teacher called, glancing around to check that they were alone, 'Alice, I wonder if I could have a word with you?'

'Of course. The school bus has left so there's nobody around,' the girl replied. 'Shall we sit?' Alice patted a bench in the mottled shade of a gum by the roadside.

'You're very special to me, you know,' Miss Kerr began, 'and I'd like to ask a favour.'

'Your wish is my command,' Alice chuckled.

'I have no children,' Miss Kerr went on, 'and since my nieces are all grown up, I was wondering if you would be my bridesmaid?'

Alice gaped. 'You're getting married at last?' she gasped. 'To?'

'To Mr Solomon, of course.'

'That's wonderful news,' Alice said. 'I'd love to be your bridesmaid. But what about your dear mother?'

Miss Kerr shook her head. 'I'm afraid that I can't look after her anymore. I've arranged for her to be cared for in a nursing home not five miles away. Provided I can see her regularly, and she can still play cards, she'll be happy. I can't be a wife and a nurse and a teacher. And I very much want to go on teaching.'

'I understand,' Alice said. 'I was just telling my Birdy, we all have to go our own ways someday – like I'm going to boarding school next year. I hope.'

'Very true,' Miss Kerr agreed. 'We must go on, mustn't we? Remember Mrs Goodenough after she lost her mother-in-law? They were so close . . .'

'Let's not be sad. Tell me, where and when is the big day? And what will you wear? What will I wear, now I think about it?'

Miss Kerr smiled. 'Well,' she said, warming to the topic, 'I don't want some la-di-dah wedding.

Colin and I are too old for that. I was wondering, do you think your dear Mr Brown would let us tie the knot in the clearing in front of his house? It's so lovely there in the forest with those ferns. What do you think he would say to that?'

Alice clapped her hands in delight. 'I'm sure he'd agree,' she said. 'I'm certain of it.'

'Then I'll write him a note and ask,' Miss Kerr said.

'But dresses?' Alice asked again. 'What about dresses?'

'We can catch the train to Melbourne and make a day of it. I'll get a suit for myself – in some soft colour, lavender, say, I don't care much for white – and something pink for you. What do you say?'

'They say that redheads should never wear pink,' Alice said. 'Is that true?'

'Tush!' Miss Kerr exclaimed. 'Who cares what they say? Who are *they* anyway? You will look beautiful in pink, never fear.'

'Okay,' Alice agreed. 'Pink it is. I quite like breaking rules. And speaking of breaking rules, can I volunteer that my mum and I make the wedding cake? Her dark fruit cake is fantastic, just ask Mr Cyril Brown – and I make the best marzipan icing. With lacy decorations. I do. Please?'

Miss Kerr turned to give Alice a hug. 'Off to boarding school to become a great success, I don't doubt, and now you're making my wedding cake. No wonder I'm proud of you.'

'But when's the big day? You haven't said.'

'Now that school's nearly over and I have time to settle Mum in, I think a week before Christmas.'

'That's just days away,' Alice said. 'We'll need to get to Melbourne pretty soon.'

'We will. There's only one drawback: flowers. The Christmas heat is always awful and while there will be summer roses, they wilt so quickly. I'm trying to think of what else would do.'

The idea came to Alice in a flash. 'Leave the bouquet to me, Miss Kerr. It will be spectacular,

I promise . . . Now I must get home to study. As you know, I have my last test tomorrow and certainly don't want to fail.'

The wedding of Miss Veronica Kerr and Mr Colin Solomon was talked about for years. Among the many reasons for this interest was the fact that, having been Miss Kerr's students, most people in the community were unaware of her full name until the padre announced it to an audible sigh of approval. And then, of course, there was the collective awe upon looking up at the cathedral-like vaults of mountain ash, the sublime shafts of sunlight beaming through the ferns, and the spirited choir of songbirds that fell silent as the white-ribboned sulky bearing the bride arrived.

Veronica Kerr looked smashing in her suit of lavender water-wave taffeta, complete with the nattiest white voile fascinator, tipped alluringly over her eyes. But no one could have predicted the

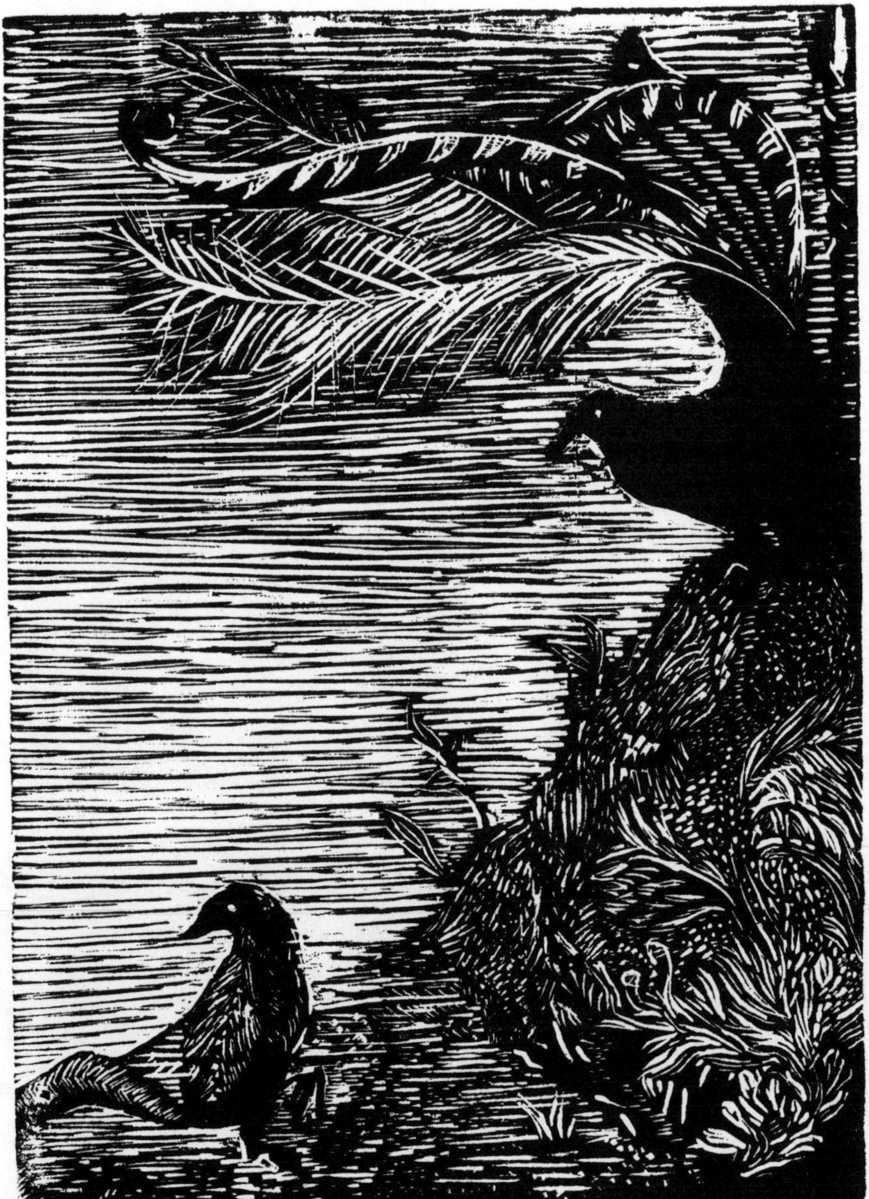

beauty of her bouquet – if that is what it could be called. Thanks to Alice, Veronica carried the very same lyrebird tail feathers, long since gathered from the forest floor by Marcella Brown, that had once graced the dim interior of the Browns' home. 'My pleasure,' Mr Brown had said when Alice asked. 'Marcella would be delighted.'

Beautiful though the bride was (and Colin Solomon looked pretty good too, in his spanking new navy blue pinstriped suit complete with a flash waistcoat tailored in matching lavender taffeta), none could outdo the beaming bridesmaid. 'She's wearing pink,' some old biddy whispered, 'and she's a redhead!'

'So?' her husband muttered.

And we will say nothing about the cake . . . well, no more than to make mention that the promised lacy decorations in dazzling white marzipan were stunning recreations of the tail feathers of a lyrebird – who would have expected that?

CHAPTER THIRTEEN

A FEW DAYS BEFORE CHRISTMAS, ERNIE DORRITT returned from a visit to the craft centre in town bearing a handful of mail. Since it was the holidays, Alice was in her bedroom reading and Gwen was sorting through timber offcuts considering which might be useful for her next sculpture.

Ernie dropped the mail on the kitchen table, whispered in Gwen's ear, then called, 'Alice, there's something out here that you might like to see . . .' He flashed an imposing monogrammed envelope before Gwen's eyes.

'What? Tell me,' Alice yelled back. 'I'm reading.'

'Don't worry,' he teased, 'we can use the paper to light the fire.'

Seconds later, the envelope was snatched from his fingers and with a 'Yahoo!', the girl ran back to her bedroom. A further 'Yahoo!' followed, even louder than the first. Only then did Alice return, her face flushed, her eyes wild, her hands pressed to her mouth, the envelope crushed between her fingers. 'I'm in!' she shouted, hugging her parents. 'I've been accepted by Lilydale Grammar – and with a two-year scholarship. I'm in!' She danced around the kitchen, alternately waving the letter in the air, then kissing it – but by the back door, facing the bush, she stopped.

'What's the matter?' her mother asked, holding her. 'Are you all right?'

Alice turned to face her parents. 'Now I'm actually leaving, I don't know if I want to. You'll be by yourselves. And who will visit Mr Brown? And who will care for Birdy? I can't go,' she wailed. 'I can't . . .'

Her father put his arms around both mother and daughter. 'For a start,' he said, his voice calm and reassuring, 'your mother and I lived here for years – yes, all by ourselves – and we didn't mope or moan. And as for Mr Cyril Brown, Alice, I just met him walking the track into town to meet his old mate Harry at the post office. They're going to the pub for lunch. Think about it: he's pushing eighty and he probably has lots of buddies that you know nothing about, as well as your Birdy, who's as close to Cyril as you are. And speaking of Birdy, he's a wild thing, and wild things adapt. He's adapted to you – to us – hasn't he? Any wild thing's dependence on humans isn't natural. Believe me, when you go, Birdy will find a mate and readapt to the bush. So stop fretting. You're a teenager and your education is your future. Make that future your own. Now show me that letter before you turn it to pulp.' And, taking the letter from her, he sat at the kitchen table to read it.

Gwen Dorritt turned to the back door and paused, looking out into the bush. Although there were tears in her eyes, she said, 'Alice, your father's right. You know how much you want a career like Sheila, the photographer . . .'

'Or Grace from the museum,' Alice added. 'I know. I've been thinking about that. I like the idea of photographing wildlife, and I *love* the idea of researching endangered species, like Grace, but I've been thinking about what she told me. She said that before she decided to specialise in endangered species she'd been doing some basic research into the study of fossils. Palaeontology, that's called. That Dr Ingram's a palaeontologist. He's the one who said it might take years to find out if I found a fern fossil or a feather fossil . . .'

'Or maybe even a fossilised lyrebird feather,' her father suggested with a knowing wink.

'Exactly!' Alice said. 'Who could hope for more? Imagine, fossilised traces of one of Birdy's ancestors still being here, in our forest, nearly at our back door!'

'I'm not sure that's very likely,' her mother said.

'But don't you see? That's what I want to find out. I'd like to be the first palaeontologist to find the fossilised feather of a lyrebird in this country. Wouldn't that be wonderful?'

'So you *do* want a job like Sheila and Grace, working outdoors, in the wild, maybe with wild things, or saving wild things?' her father asked.

Overcome with excitement, Alice pressed her hands to her cheeks. 'Or discovering traces of wild things – *prehistoric* traces. Imagine that!'

'But you can't do that if you're stuck here,' her mother reminded her. 'It's all right for your father and me, we make stuff. We get by, but we enjoy what we do. And you will too. I tell you what, let's give Cyril a chance to catch up with Mr Shields, then how about you visit and tell him your good news. And it *is* good news. The very best news. Congratulations. Ernie, have you congratulated your wonderful daughter?'

Ernie Dorritt got to his feet. 'Great offer, Alice,' he said, 'pity there wasn't a few quid in it for us.'

Smiling broadly, he gathered his family in his arms again.

Late that afternoon, Alice walked to Mr Brown's house, her scholarship offer in hand. Bounding up the front steps, she knocked, calling, 'Mr B. It's Alice. I have news.'

The house was silent.

That's odd, she thought, and called again, 'Mr Brown, it's Alice.'

Still nothing.

Maybe he's not home yet, she thought. Opening the door, she called again.

Nothing.

I'll come back later, she decided but as she closed the door behind her she caught a sound – a sob, was it? – and, half entering she called, 'Mr B, are you there?'

'In here,' a voice answered, though she didn't recognise it as her friend's.

'Where's here?'

'My bedroom,' came the reply. 'First on your right.'

'Can I come in?'

When no one replied, Alice entered. She'd never been in Mr Brown's bedroom before. She'd never been shown that room, so she hesitated, uncomfortable.

The door was ajar. Glimpsing a pair of boots lying on the coverlet of a brass bed, Alice knocked. 'Are you all right?' she called, her hand on the glass door knob. 'Is it okay for me to come in?'

'Okay,' came the response.

Alice entered the room. The first thing she saw was Mr Brown lying fully dressed on a white cambric bedspread – muddy boots and all.

'Mr Brown,' Alice gasped, astonished. 'Whatever's the matter?'

When he didn't answer, she glanced around the room. Maybe he's been sick, she thought. Maybe he had too much to drink with Harry – but the room was neat as a new pin: the lace curtains covering the French doors hung in perfect folds, a massive silky oak dressing table complete with oval mirror sat solid in the corner to her right and on it, still neatly arranged, sat a crystal tray carrying a hair brush, hand mirror and comb, all in tortoiseshell. Marcella's, Alice thought. Untouched . . . then realising that she was gripping one of the uprights of the brass four-poster bed, she stepped back, aware of her proximity to the man lying upon it.

'Mr Brown,' she said, 'can I help?'

Her friend turned his head, but only to face the wall away from her, then slowly, he patted the bedside table beside him.

'Read that,' he muttered into a pillow.

'That?' Alice replied, not understanding.

'The letter. There.' He patted the table again and Alice saw a sheet of paper beneath his palm, and an envelope, torn open.

'Are you sure?' she asked, hesitating.

Cyril Brown sobbed, his hand covering his face.

Alice made her way around the bed and picked up the paper.

'Don't read it out,' he said. 'I couldn't bear it. Read it to yourself and leave. Please . . .'

Alice took the letter to the window to read by the light. It began,

Dear Sir, we trust that this note will find you. The Post Office in your town was the only forwarding address available to us. It is our sad duty to inform you that your son, Ronald Brown, was drowned in a boating accident in Victoria Harbour in the Port of Hong Kong a week ago. Ronald Brown (we believe that was his name, though he often used an alias) was a regular tenant of a boarding house that we conduct for sailors. We understand that he was employed in the jade industry, trading carvings and other exotic curiosities to Westerners. We sincerely regret your loss.
Yours, and a signature followed.

Alice placed the note back on the table and sat on the edge of the bed, her left hand reaching out to grip Mr Brown's.

He pulled away. 'Alice,' he said, 'please leave me. This is too much to bear . . .' and reluctantly, the girl left, closing the door behind her.

Mrs Dorritt listened while Alice wept. 'He asked me to leave,' she said through her tears. 'After all this time, Mr Brown asked me to leave.'

'Alice,' her mother said, 'he has just learnt of the death of his son. And he's only recently lost his wife. He's not angry at you. He's grieving. Try to understand.'

'And remember, when Marcella died, he didn't tell us. He bore her loss alone. People grieve in different ways,' her father explained. 'I'd say that he needs his solitude – that's how he grieves. Okay?'

'But we're good friends,' Alice said. 'And good friends share.'

Her parents exchanged glances over their daughter's head.

'Alice,' her mother said, 'you are good friends – we know that, and Mr Brown knows that but you're a fourteen-year-old girl, and he's an elderly man. I'm certain that he respects you. I'm also certain that he knows his own mind.'

'Give him a few days, then drop by to see how he's going? Agreed?' her father suggested.

'I'll make some meals for him,' her mother said. 'And some bread. And cake. You can take that over. Right?'

Alice nodded, wiping her eyes. 'Right,' she sniffed. 'But only two days, no more.'

The following morning, Ernie Dorritt returned from town with another envelope addressed to Alice.

'Whatever can this be?' the girl wondered, opening the flap carefully. 'It's got something hard inside.' And when she withdrew the contents, all was revealed: 'There's a note from Sheila Kavanagh,' she said, 'and a photo. A photo of me and Mr B at the fossil site. Sheila must have snapped it before she came over to share our lunch. Look . . .' Alice held the photo out for her parents to see.

'Wonderful,' her mother said. 'Now that should cheer you up.'

Mr Dorritt reached across the table. He smiled when he saw the image but then his expression changed. 'Um . . . I think you should look more closely, Miss Alice. This photo bears a secret. See?' and he gave the photo back.

Alice looked very hard. 'What am I looking for?' she wanted to know. 'And where?'

Mr Dorritt winked at his wife who appeared as puzzled as Alice. 'You and Mr B are sitting side by side on a log, right? Now look among the bushes between your shoulders. Look very carefully . . .'

Alice turned the image to the light from the kitchen window and squealed with delight. 'It's

Birdy. It's Birdy sneaked in between us. See, Mum? It's wonderful. The three of us together. Sheila said she wanted a photo of a lyrebird and she got one – by accident maybe – but she got one! I must show Mr B. I must . . .' and she turned to go.

'Two days, you said,' her father reminded her. 'And it's not two days till tomorrow. Those were your rules. Remember?'

If Alice could possibly have forgotten to visit Mr Brown, a very clear reminder was delivered to her bedroom first thing the next morning when Birdy came tapping at her glass. 'What are you doing here?' she mumbled, sitting up in bed. 'It's not your day. You came yesterday.'

Birdy tapped even harder.

'*Schmak! Schmak!*'

'What?' Alice demanded, crossing to the window. 'Do you want me to feed you? Is that it?' But as soon as she approached, the bird backed

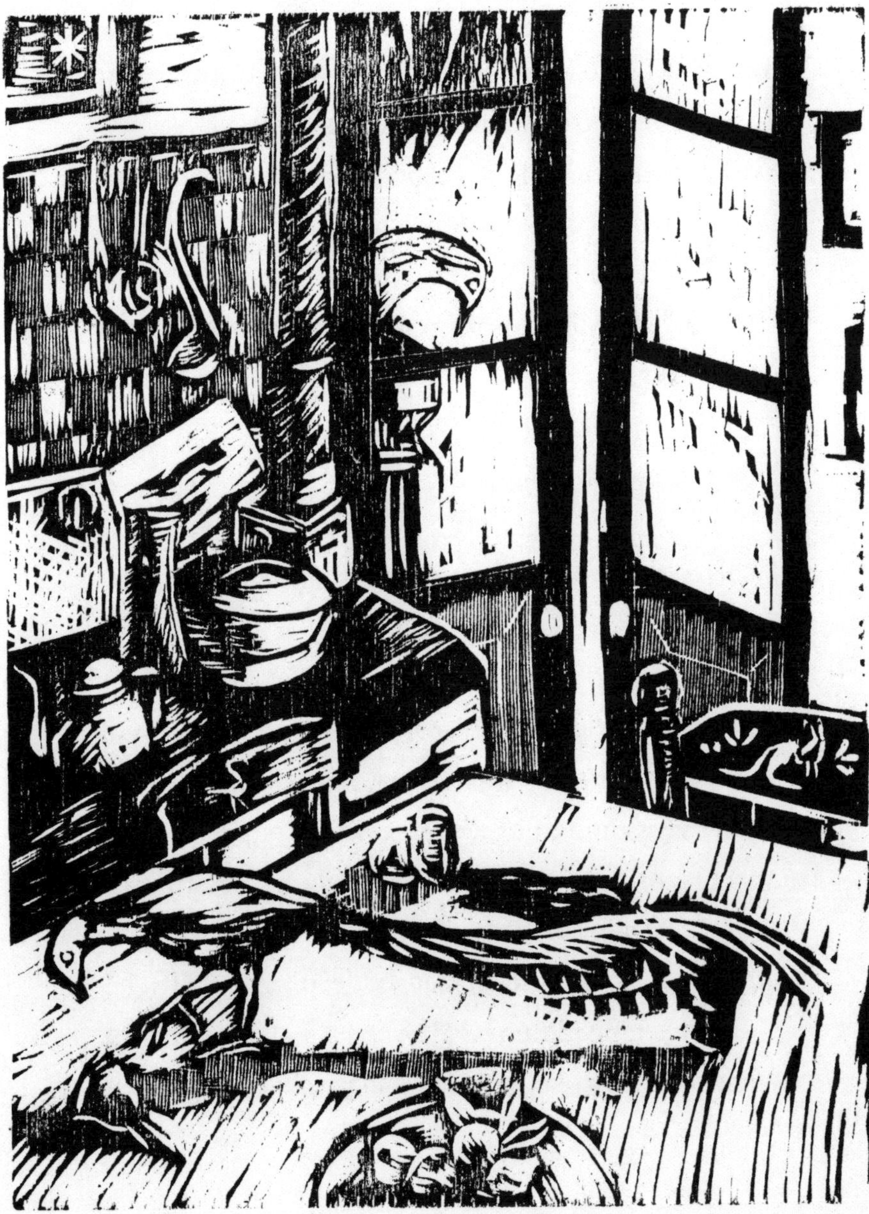

away. 'What?' she asked again. 'What are you trying to tell me?' And then an idea dawned. 'It's your day at Mr B's,' she breathed. 'You've been there and you want me to go back with you.'

The bird blinked.

At last Alice understood. 'And you want me to go now!'

'I'm off to Mr Brown's,' she called from outside her parents' bedroom door.

'I'll pack some food,' Mrs Dorritt answered. 'Wait a minute,' but their daughter was gone.

Alice hurried up Mr Brown's front steps and saw that the front door was closed, so she turned right onto the verandah and looked in through the lace curtains of the French doors of the main bedroom. She could not see clearly but there was Mr Brown, all tucked up in bed, evidently sleeping soundly.

Alice tapped on the glass. As she did, she heard what seemed to be an echo. Birdy was tapping too.

Mr Brown slept on.

Alice tapped louder.

Birdy *schmaked* louder.

Mr Brown slept on.

'I don't like this,' Alice said. 'I'm going in.'

Opening the bedroom door very slowly, Alice peeped inside. Mr Brown lay very still, his arms folded on his chest, his hands clasped on the bedspread. Through the lace curtains, she caught a glimpse of Birdy, strutting up and down outside.

'Mr Brown,' Alice whispered. 'Mr Brown . . .' but when she came up close, she froze. *He's not asleep*, she thought. Without a second thought she hurried to the dressing table, picked up Marcella's tortoiseshell hand mirror, and held it to his lips.

Nothing.

No mist.

No breath.

'Goodbye, my friend,' Alice breathed. 'Goodbye . . .'

On the day she left for boarding school, Alice's parents drove her to the railway station in the ancient Model T Ford. When they reached the turn-off to the Browns', she said, 'Can we stop here for a minute? Please?'

Her father pulled up. Alice got out and looked towards the house, remembering the first time she had taken that path. As she turned, Birdy appeared. He looked up at her and blinked then, in a moment, he bowed and, for the first time, spread his glorious tail feathers in full display. Alice knelt before him. 'I have to leave the forest, Birdy,' she said. 'I need to face my future, but I will never forget the past – neither the people, the forest, nor you – and that's a promise.'

AUTHOR'S NOTE

THE LYREBIRD IS AN ICONIC CREATURE OF THE Australian forest. Other than the sublime beauty of its plumage, the bird's ability to mimic any sound – of a machine, of another bird, of another animal or human – establishes it as a natural phenomenon. Ambrose Pratt (1933) and Alex Chisholm (1960) were two researchers of Australian wildlife who wrote detailed studies of lyrebirds' behaviour, their natural habitat and their extraordinary social attachment to humans. I bought the books, listed on the following page, from an archival book supplier in my hometown of Maleny in the 1990s. Maleny is set among the subtropical forests of the Blackall Range in the Sunshine Coast hinterland in Queensland. Chisholm's book tells of how the lyrebird once populated the forests not far from my home (Chisholm, p. 83). For this reason, it has long been my intention to use these books as the basis for an original story. My other reason for writing this book is also sad, but my message is urgent. Tragically, non-indigenous, introduced species such as foxes and cats have destroyed the lyrebird population in the Blackall Range. Like Ambrose Pratt in the 1930s, I have written this book in the hope that I can educate people regarding these incredible creatures, ensuring that those lyrebirds which survive in other Australian forests 'will be safe' (Pratt, p. 79).

References:
Chisholm, AH 1960, *The Romance of the Lyrebird*, Angus and Robertson, Sydney.
Pratt, A 1933, *The Lore of the Lyrebird*, Robertson and Mullins, Melbourne.

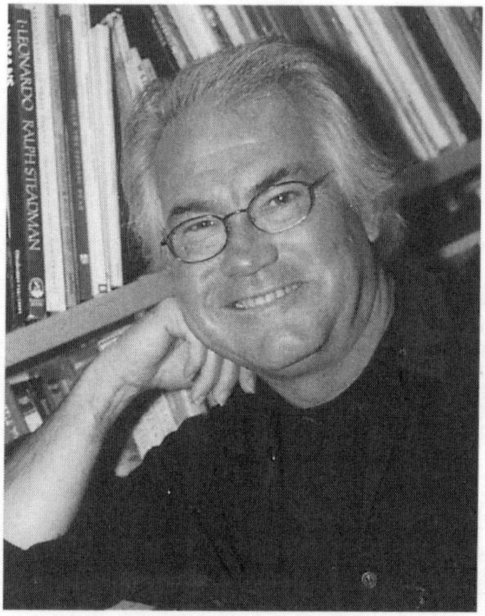
LEONARDO
RALPH STEADMAN

Gary Crew writes short stories, novels and picture books. Gary is Professor of Creative Writing at the University of the Sunshine Coast, Queensland. During his publishing career of over 30 years Gary has won the Children's Book Council of Australia's Book of the Year four times, twice for novels and twice for his picture books, the New South Wales Premier's Award, the Victorian Premier's Award, the American Children's Book of Distinction, the Aurealis Best Children's Short Fiction, the Wilderness Society's Award for Environmental Writing, and the Royal Zoological Society Whitley Award. Gary lives on the waterfront of subtropical Bribie Island. When he is not writing or lecturing, he loves to walk by the sea or read.

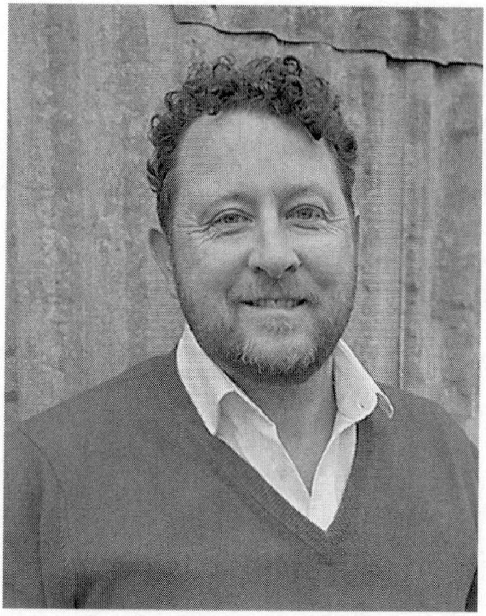

Julian Laffan creates art and illustration in a rusty old shed in the historic town of Braidwood, New South Wales. In between making woodcuts he walks to school to be the Assistant Principal at St. Bede's. With Natasha and their son Orlando, he spends his holidays bushwalking, wandering the streets of Paris or trying to ride horses in Mongolia.

For a bonus image from *Leaving the Lyrebird Forest* visit julian-laffan.squarespace.com

hachette
CHILDREN'S BOOKS

If you would like to find out more about Hachette Children's Books, our authors, upcoming events and new releases you can visit our website, Facebook or follow us on Twitter:

hachettechildrens.com.au
twitter.com/HCBoz
facebook.com/hcboz

Teachers notes are available from the Hachette Australia website:
www.hachette.com.au/teachers-and-librarians